014

REKI KAWAHARA ABEC BEE-PEE

SWORD ART ONLINE

Alicization uniting

SAO SWORD ART ONLINE

"I don't remember, and I don't care."

Eugeo § The first resident of this world whom Kirito met. He has joined Kirito in seeking out the top floor of Central Cathedral on a quest to rescue his childhood friend Alice until...

"Eugeo...do you remember the person who taught you that move?"

— Kirito § A boy who found himself within the mysterious fantasy realm known as the Underworld. He is striving toward the top floor of Central Cathedral for the means to escape back to reality.

"It can't be...!"

Alice Synthesis Thirty § The girl Eugeo has been seeking. But after undergoing the Synthesis Ritual, she is now an Integrity Knight who serves Administrator.

"Is…is this…?!"

"Release Recollection!!"

Administrator § A girl born within the Underworld with such rare talent that she unlocked and mastered the system commands on her own. She is the pontifex, the ruler of all humanity, and resides within the top floor of Central Cathedral.

"My sword…is already…broken."

TOP FLOOR OF CENTRAL CATHEDRAL

Crystals Embedded in Ceiling

100F
Chamber of the Gods

96–99F
Senate
VS Chudelkin

95F
Morning Star Lookout

90F
Great Bath
VS Bercouli Synthesis One

80F
Cloudtop Garden
VS Alice Synthesis Thirty

Top Floor of Central Cathedral

The residence of Administrator, the pontifex of the Axiom Church and ruler of the Underworld's human realm. An elevating platform goes from here to the ninety-ninth floor via a hole in the carpet on the south side of the room. This domed chamber is much larger than the ninety-ninth floor, at about forty mels across. It is surrounded by glass windows and offers a full view of the starry night sky. The windows are separated by golden pillars, each featuring a gigantic decorative sword. Tiny crystals are embedded in the white domed ceiling, forming a vast mural that depicts the gods, an enormous dragon, and humankind in fine detail. The floor is covered with thick carpet, and in the center of the chamber is a vast round bed where Administrator sleeps.

Map Illustration: Tatsuya Kurusu

SWORD ART ONLINE

Alicization uniting

VOLUME 14

Reki Kawahara

abec

bee-pee

NEW YORK

SWORD ART ONLINE, Volume 14: ALICIZATION UNITING
REKI KAWAHARA

Translation by Stephen Paul
Cover art by abec

SWORD ART ONLINE Vol.14
©REKI KAWAHARA 2014
First published in Japan in 2014 by KADOKAWA CORPORATION, Tokyo.
English translation rights arranged with KADOKAWA CORPORATION, Tokyo,
through Tuttle-Mori Agency, Inc., Tokyo.

English translation © 2018 by Yen Press, LLC

Yen On
1290 Avenue of the Americas
New York, NY 10104

Visit us at yenpress.com
facebook.com/yenpress
twitter.com/yenpress
yenpress.tumblr.com
instagram.com/yenpress

First Yen On Edition: August 2018

Yen On is an imprint of Yen Press, LLC.
The Yen On name and logo are trademarks of Yen Press, LLC.

Library of Congress Cataloging-in-Publication Data
Names: Kawahara, Reki, author. | Abec, 1985– illustrator. | Paul, Stephen, translator.
Title: Sword art online / Reki Kawahara, abec ; translation, Stephen Paul.
Description: First Yen On edition. | New York, NY : Yen On, 2014–
Identifiers: LCCN 2014001175 | ISBN 9780316371247 (v. 1 : pbk.) |
    ISBN 9780316376815 (v. 2 : pbk.) | ISBN 9780316296427 (v. 3 : pbk.) |
    ISBN 9780316296434 (v. 4 : pbk.) | ISBN 9780316296441 (v. 5 : pbk.) |
    ISBN 9780316296458 (v. 6 : pbk.) | ISBN 9780316390408 (v. 7 : pbk.) |
    ISBN 9780316390415 (v. 8 : pbk.) | ISBN 9780316390422 (v. 9 : pbk.) |
    ISBN 9780316390439 (v. 10 : pbk.) | ISBN 9780316390446 (v. 11 : pbk.) |
    ISBN 9780316390453 (v. 12 : pbk.) | ISBN 9780316390460 (v. 13 : pbk.) |
    ISBN 9780316390484 (v. 14 : pbk.)
Subjects: | CYAC: Science fiction. | BISAC: FICTION / Science Fiction / Adventure.
Classification: pz7.K1755Ain 2014 | DDC [Fic]—dc23
LC record available at https://lccn.loc.gov/2014001175

ISBNs: 978-0-316-39048-4 (paperback)
       978-0-316-56106-8 (ebook)

10 9 8 7 6 5 4 3 2 1

LSC-C

Printed in the United States of America

"THIS MIGHT BE A GAME, BUT IT'S NOT SOMETHING YOU PLAY."

—Akihiko Kayaba, *Sword Art Online* programmer

SWORD ART ONLINE
Alicization uniting

Reki Kawahara

abec

bee-pee

Integrity Knights. Or, occasionally, Integrators.

They were the most powerful of servants, possessing finely honed swordsmanship, high-level sacred arts, and even at-will use of fearsome Perfect Weapon Control abilities.

For three hundred long years, these knights had been the force upholding the law and order of the four empires of man, as well as the rule of the Axiom Church—but the knighthood itself was stunningly small. As suggested by the name of the most recently inducted knight, Eldrie Synthesis Thirty-One, there were barely over thirty of them.

But rather than diminishing the dignity and potency of the knighthood, their small number only enhanced it. A group smaller than a full raid party in games like *SAO* or *ALO* had kept the lands of humanity safe from encroachers in the Dark Territory for all these years.

I, Kirito, once known as "Beater" or the "Black Swordsman" but now an elite disciple at the North Centoria Imperial Swordcraft Academy, armed with nothing more than my trusty blade and an even more trusted companion, had launched into battle against this band of Integrity Knights. Our rebellion wasn't by design but rather was the consequence of escaping from jail—because once we had drawn our blades against the Axiom Church, the ultimate ruling body of the land, there was no way out but forward.

Eldrie Synthesis Thirty-One, user of the Frostscale Whip.

Deusolbert Synthesis Seven, user of the Conflagration Bow.

Fanatio Synthesis Two, user of the Heaven-Piercing Blade and her Four Whirling Blades.

Alice Synthesis Thirty, user of the Osmanthus Blade.

We had made our way up the grand staircase of the Axiom Church's Central Cathedral, just barely besting these knights and their almighty weapons, which were known as Divine Objects. Needless to say, it wasn't my skill alone that had paved the way.

The craftsman Sadore in Centoria had taken an entire year to fashion a branch of the demonic Gigas Cedar into a single black sword for me.

The sage Cardinal had provided me with rest, food, vast knowledge of the world, and the Perfect Weapon Control skill needed to fight back against the knights.

And most of all, I had my friend Eugeo, who had been at my side for two long years, ever since we left the distant village of Rulid.

I had taught Eugeo the One-Handed Sword skills of the Aincrad style, but he had given me so much more in return. The only reason I'd survived my unexpected plunge from the real world into the unfamiliar Underworld was the help, encouragement, and guidance of Eugeo.

At the eightieth floor of Central Cathedral, I was separated from my partner. In the midst of a fierce battle, the Integrity Knight Alice and I punched a hole in the outer wall of the tower and tumbled out.

I took great pains to convince Alice to stay her sword, but over the course of an entire night, we managed to climb the sheer wall of the tower until we at last reentered the building on the ninety-fifth floor. I raced up the stairs, certain that Eugeo was ahead of me now, and met a creepy man named Prime Senator Chudelkin. I chased him up to the ninety-ninth floor, just one floor below the chamber of Administrator, pontifex of the Axiom Church and supreme ruler of humanity.

It was in this room, featureless aside from the staircase leading back down to the senate floors and the levitating platform up to the hundredth floor, that I was reunited with my partner.

But he was no longer the simple, purehearted young man that I knew.

Now he was Eugeo Synthesis Thirty-Two, clad in the silver armor of an Integrity Knight.

CHAPTER TWELVE

1

Both Eugeo's Blue Rose Sword and my black blade carved light-green trails in the darkened chamber.

The paths formed a perfect symmetry. This was to be expected, as we launched into identical skills simultaneously, including the charging skill Sonic Leap. The timing was perfectly aligned, such that the sword tips reached the peak of their curve, flashing brighter to indicate the attack power was at its maximum potential, at precisely the same moment before silver and black edges collided.

I didn't just execute the technique. I used the tension in my feet, rotation of my body, and swing of my arms as three separate accelerative forces on the attack. Even so, Eugeo's Sonic Leap wasn't even a microsecond slower than mine. He had pushed his as far as it could go, just like I had. And I hadn't even fully taught him how to do that yet.

Somehow, when I hadn't been paying attention, Eugeo had kept patiently, stubbornly swinging away. Hundreds of times, every single day, until he could hear the voice of the sword.

"...How?" I grunted under my breath as our swords clashed at their intersection point. "How did you lose to the Synthesis Ritual? The reason you studied the blade...the reason you left Rulid for Centoria was to take back your childhood friend Alice. Right?"

"..."

Eugeo stood firm, blocking my sword. As he'd warned before we started, he had nothing more to say to me—his lips were shut tight. I felt like I saw a glimmer in his green eyes the moment he heard the name Alice, but whatever that was, it was instantly swallowed by darkness. Perhaps it was nothing more than a trick of the eyes, caused by the green glow coming from the swords.

If our stalemate continued for a few seconds longer, the Sonic Leaps would expire, ushering us into a furious close-range swordfight. At that point, I wouldn't have the time to think. I used the brief recess to furiously spur my mind onward.

Integrity Knights were created through direct operation of their souls, in what was called the Synthesis Ritual. It involved extracting a crystal of memories from the subject's mind and replacing it with a device that forced their loyalty, an object called a Piety Module.

The moment Eldrie had heard his mother's name, he'd become unstable, and the Piety Module had begun to emerge from his forehead. That meant that in order to make him an Integrity Knight, Administrator had stolen his memories of his mother.

The other knights must've lost similarly precious memories. For Deusolbert, it was likely the memory of his wife. For Fanatio and Bercouli, I couldn't be sure yet, but I imagined it was either families or lovers.

So who would it be for Alice? The golden knight was back against the wall, watching the fight between Eugeo and me. The most probable answer was her little sister, Selka, who was still living back in Rulid. When I had casually dropped Selka's name while we were resting on the terrace ledge outside the tower, Alice had reacted violently. She'd cried at the mention of her sister and even sworn rebellion against the Axiom Church.

But the mention of Selka's name didn't cause Alice's Piety Module to become unstable, as far as I could tell. That was either because she'd been an Integrity Knight for six years already or because the stolen memories weren't actually of Selka.

Assuming my conjectures about these matters were accurate, then whose memory did Administrator steal from Eugeo?

Not far from where we stood locked in combat was the levitating platform, which Chudelkin had used to flee to the floor above, and which I'd summoned back down. There was a hole in the ceiling about three feet across. It had to be Administrator's chamber through there, but it was pitch-black through the hole. If she was up there right now, I couldn't tell.

But just an hour ago, she had "synthesized" Eugeo there—stealing his most precious memories. But of whom?

There was only one answer I could imagine. It was the girl he'd been chasing after for eight years, ever since Deusolbert took her away when she was a child. Alice Zuberg, who was now Alice Synthesis Thirty.

Then why did Eugeo have no reaction toward Alice, who was standing in the very same room with us while we dueled? Eldrie's module nearly fell out just at the mention of his mother's name. If his instability was a factor of how little time he'd spent as an Integrity Knight—well, Eugeo had been one for barely an hour. He should've had an even more violent reaction the instant he saw Alice.

But this Eugeo was completely closed off from the world. If it wasn't memories of Alice that had been removed from him, then who—or what—did Administrator take away?

At that moment, the shine from the two clashing sword skills faded.

Without the propulsion that the system assistance gave them, the white and black blades recoiled from each other. As sparks flew, I clenched my teeth and Eugeo looked as impassive as ever. We brandished our swords for new attacks.

"Yaaah!"

"…!"

With simultaneous cries—one voiced and one mute—we launched high left-handed swings with perfect synchronization. The blades clashed and recoiled, and next was a swipe from the right side. The edges clanged and slid, leading to a downward left swing. This, too, was firmly caught.

As we settled into our second stalemate, I couldn't help but marvel. Our swords might have identical stats, but the people who wielded them did not. I was lighter, with regular clothes, while Eugeo wore heavy plate armor. He was lugging around many times the weight I was, yet his attacks were coming with the exact same speed. Either turning into an Integrity Knight bumped up his strength, or this was the effect of that "Incarnate" thing Alice had mentioned just before the fight.

I knew that this world contained some systems that couldn't be explained with the logic of all the other VRMMO worlds I'd experienced to this point. Invisible forces like willpower and imagination could, at times, produce effects beyond that of even high-level system commands.

Becoming an Integrity Knight had taken away Eugeo's memories and emotions, but his willpower was cold and sharp. Before we started fighting, he had summoned the Blue Rose Sword I possessed to his hand as though through telekinesis—an ability Alice had called Incarnate Arms.

What was actually in Eugeo's heart now? It was the determination to take Alice back from the Church that drove him to want to be an Integrity Knight in the first place. What kind of will was now filling the enormous void left in its place?

I couldn't imagine that it was all just loyalty to the Axiom Church and its pontifex, etched into his soul. I didn't want to believe that; there was no way the Blue Rose Sword could withstand every last ounce of my black sword's strength with that kind of artificial willpower.

Somewhere within those icy cold eyes, something was still burning. I had to believe in that. And if there was one way to summon that forth, it had to be…

"…Eugeo," I whispered, pushing against the sword with all my strength, "maybe you don't remember this anymore…but you and I never actually got to fight with everything we have, before."

"…"

Eugeo's eyes, which had once shone a brilliant green, were now dark and dull. I stared into them, willing them to respond.

"On the journey from Rulid to Centoria, and while we were at Swordcraft Academy, I asked myself the same question many times: Who would win if we crossed blades for real? And to be honest…I felt like one day, you would surpass me."

Eugeo returned my gaze without blinking. In fact, he didn't return it—his eyes were like closed shutters. I was nothing but an intruder who needed to be eliminated. If I showed him even an instant of weakness, he would strike. But I still delivered the conclusion of my speech, believing that *something* would get through to him.

"…But now is not that time. You've forgotten about me, about Alice, about Tiese and Ronie, and even about Cardinal. You can't beat me. And I'm going to prove that to you."

As soon as the words had left my mouth, I stopped breathing and willed the strength of every muscle in my body into my sword. Fine wrinkles appeared on Eugeo's brow as he attempted to push back.

At that instant, I pulled back.

Zshang! The blades clashed, producing a line of sparks in the gloom. The shift in momentum pushed me backward and caused Eugeo to lean forward.

If I tried to steady myself, I'd be a sitting duck for Eugeo. Instead, I pushed into the momentum and let my back fall toward the floor. Out of the corner of my eye, I spotted Alice reaching across her body for the Osmanthus Blade, certain that I had just lost.

But her decision was coming three seconds too early. Victory or defeat would be determined by whether my strategy was successful or not—or how well Eugeo truly understood the Aincrad style.

Just before my back hit the floor, I kicked upward with my right foot. The toe of my boot shone, lighting Eugeo's chin from below.

"Yaaaah!"

I spun backward, the angle tight. It was Aincrad-style martial arts, the backflip-kick skill Crescent Moon. This handy move, which you could activate while falling backward, had saved my life on numerous occasions in the old *SAO*. I hadn't used it in combat or practice since coming to the Underworld, but the movement was etched into my muscles—and most importantly, I'd never shown it to Eugeo.

On the other hand, I *had* shown him martial arts with fists or shoulders. He'd shown proficiency with it, too. He could do the simple punching skill Flash Blow, as well as three parts of Meteor Break, the high-level combination of body blows and slashes.

If he had discovered the existence of kicking attacks in his own time, or even just suspected their existence, he was going to evade my Crescent Moon. And the downside of this attack was that it had an extremely long recovery after it had been dodged. If I missed, I would be helpless against his merciless blade.

This is it, Eugeo!

My right foot closed in on my opponent's gorget. Even in this situation, Eugeo's eyes were full of impassive frost. He twisted his torso without changing his expression, attempting to curve away from my foot. But the momentum that had pulled him forward when I fell backward was still a factor. My glowing toe shot toward his defenseless chin.

"…!"

Air shot from Eugeo's mouth. The arm holding the Blue Rose Sword swiped sideways with ferocious force. But no matter how hard he swung, my leg was faster. If I just focused on connecting, I would reach…

No.

Eugeo wasn't attempting a counterattack. He was using not the blade of the sword but its pommel and aiming it not at my body but at my leg: a backhand pommel strike. It was an utterly practical movement, one that would never exist in the Underworld, where graceful solemnity ruled all concerns of swordfighting. Even in the old *SAO*, only the most savvy of veteran PvP players could pull off such a tactic.

He could change the trajectory of the Crescent Moon by nudging it from the side. So where did I aim?

"_____!"

I gritted my teeth and did everything in my power to hold back the kick. But if I pulled too hard, the skill would fumble, leaving me helpless. I had to delay the progress for what felt to me like a quarter of a second so that Eugeo's hand would pass first.

Now!

A hard crash erupted.

Rather than hitting Eugeo's throat as originally planned, my Crescent Moon got him on the back of the hand that held his sword. Like the other Integrity Knights, he wore tough gauntlets, so this wouldn't damage his hand—but it had the exact effect I was hoping for.

Eugeo's right hand bounced upward, knocking the Blue Rose Sword from his grasp. It spun upward and embedded itself in the marble ceiling, which I spotted out of the corner of my eye. I squeezed my sword, readying myself to attack once my backflip followed through and I landed on my feet again.

The sole of my shoe—the glow of the attack fading—touched solid ground. I bent my knees, absorbing the impact, and launched myself before I could straighten up or fall again. My left foot soared forward, pushing me right at the unarmed Eugeo's breastplate, where I would deliver the simple Slant attack at an upward diagonal from the left—

"_____?!"

As I rose, leaning at an extreme forward angle in the process of activating my skill, Eugeo's left hand reached out with the fingers glowing green. Just before my sword could bite into that shining armor, I heard Eugeo announce, "Burst Element."

Five separate wind elements burst from his fingers, enveloping me in an explosive gust of wind. As it was just a simple release, it didn't inflict any pain, just force, but that was enough to buffet me into the air like a scrap of cloth.

"Arrgh...!" I grunted, spreading my arms in a desperate attempt to maintain balance. If I hit the wall headfirst, I'd lose over 10 percent of my life. Instead, I managed to spin myself so that my feet were pointed toward the onrushing surface.

The instant I landed, a tremendous shudder ran through me from feet to head, pressing me to the wall until eventually the numbness subsided and I could get back down to the ground. I looked up and saw that Eugeo had been similarly pushed toward the opposite wall, but the extra weight of his armor kept him on the ground. He rose to a standing position again, his face almost obnoxiously calm.

I scrambled to my feet after him and heard a soft voice from my right say, "Is that really Eugeo, your partner?"

It was Alice, who was standing at the wall and watching the fight, as I had asked her to do. I sent the briefest of glances toward the knight in golden armor and hissed back, "What do you mean? You were the one who said he was synthesized, right?".

"Yes, I did...but...I'm not sure how to say this," she mumbled, strangely hesitant. "For being freshly synthesized, he is far too skilled in our ways of combat. Between the Incarnate Arms he used before the fight and this wind-element technique, nothing about him seems new or inexperienced."

"...So you don't just automatically know these things when you get turned into an Integrity Knight?" I asked, just to be sure. Despite the tense circumstances, I couldn't help but hunch my shoulders in embarrassment when she snapped at me.

"The knighthood's tools do not simply appear out of thin air! It takes long periods of training with weapon techniques and sacred arts to be able to use them—to say nothing of Incarnate abilities and Perfect Weapon Control!"

"Ah. R-right. But then...what was that all about just now...? I didn't think Eugeo was capable of creating five elements on one hand yet…"

"Which is *why* I was asking you if that was really Eugeo!"

"…"

I pursed my lips, staring down the knight in silver armor as he strode calmly toward me.

Just above us, on the hundredth floor of Central Cathedral, was Administrator, who, along with Cardinal in the Great Library, was the ultimate wielder of sacred arts. She could already alter the memories of people, so perhaps she could also arrange an imposter who was physically identical to the real thing. Yet…

"…It's Eugeo," I rasped.

His eyes were dull, his cheeks were pale, and there was no hint of mirth around his mouth, but the Integrity Knight was still none other than my best friend from Rulid. I'd made plenty of mistakes in the Underworld, but I was absolutely certain of this one.

How was it that the newest Integrity Knight could wield skills that stunned even Alice, who was third in their rankings? I didn't know. Neither did I know how the forced synthesis process took less than an hour for him, when it traditionally lasted three days and nights.

But no matter how much of a freakish occurrence this might be, there was no arguing with the reality of the situation. I had only one course of action: put everything into my sword and swing it. That was all.

I sucked in a deep breath, exhaled, and clutched the black blade. Eugeo stopped in the middle of the round room, perhaps sensing my determination, and extended his right hand. Those invisible Incarnate Arms reached out and plucked his longsword from the ceiling, returning it to their master's hand.

The Blue Rose Sword would never obey an imposter.

Eugeo deftly spun the impossibly heavy Divine Object and snapped it, still at chest height. There was no opening to exploit.

"Shall I try him?" Alice whispered.

"Don't be stupid," I snapped back, brandishing my own weapon. Eugeo and Alice had grown up together as friends in the village of Rulid, though neither of them could remember it now. I couldn't allow them to fight—and more importantly, it was *my* job to wake Eugeo up.

Alice had exploded with fury when I had called her stupid while we hung from the outside wall of the cathedral, but now she just took a step back and folded her arms, a sign that she would not interfere, even if it meant my defeat.

"...Thank you," I murmured, summoning all my focus to the task at hand.

I was going to forget every unnecessary thing for the sake of the battle ahead. I'd be one with my sword, utilizing every possible trick I knew. There was no way I could beat Eugeo the Integrity Knight otherwise—and no way I could speak to my friend's heart, which still beat somewhere beneath that thick metal armor.

The black tip of my sword rang softly. It was like the echo of that rumble of distant thunder on the day we started our journey two years ago, arriving through the mists of time.

Please, partner. I'll give you a name once all the fighting's done... so for now, give me strength, I pleaded with the trusty weapon in my right hand. When I was done, I took a deep breath, steadying myself.

All sounds, scenery, and even sensations faded away. The only things in the world were me, my blade, Eugeo, and the Blue Rose Sword. The moment I'd been fearing deep in my subconscious for the past two years had finally arrived.

Here I come, Eugeo!!

With a silent roar, I lunged across the floor.

Eugeo held his pose, waiting for my strike.

He was a fully adept practitioner of both the Aincrad style of swordcraft and elite sacred arts—mere trickery was meaningless against him. I sped across fifty feet of space and used all that momentum for an overhead strike from the right.

Eugeo stomped so hard he might have cracked the floor, unleashing a two-handed upward swing from his own right.

Black and white blades clashed, resulting in a bright flash of light. Our weapons bounced back, but I calculated there wasn't enough room to try a sword skill. I moved my left hand to the pommel for a two-handed grip. Without fighting against the momentum of the heavy blade, I reached an overhand stance with the shortest arc possible.

"Yaaaah!"

I expelled all my breath and swung downward. Assuming the specs of the sword and wielder alike were identical for both combatants, it was impossible to perfectly parry a direct downward swing at full strength with either a side or a diagonal swing. The only ways to stop it were to use the same attack and expect a mutual defeat or to evade the path of the sword.

But after his strike to the right, Eugeo's sword was still fully extended in that direction. Because his center of gravity was tilted there, too, he couldn't instantly jump back. This time I would land my blow!

I cast aside all distractions, focusing only on making it as quick and fierce a swing as possible. The tip of the black blade caught the armored left shoulder of my target. No matter how high priority the Integrity Knight armor was, it wasn't tough enough to deflect a blow from a divine weapon without harm.

The sword bit into the metal with a high-pitched screech and continued downward after the briefest moment of resistance. A stream of light ran from Eugeo's left shoulder near his neck to the breastplate.

A moment later, the heavy armor buckled and broke with a sound like shattering glass. The pieces of metal spun into the air, mixed with red spray. It didn't feel very deep, but my sword had undeniably gouged Eugeo's body.

The moment I recognized that I'd hurt my friend, I felt a terrible cutting pain in the same spot. I couldn't help but grimace with agony, but there was no stopping now. When my vertical swing reached the floor, I flipped my wrists and used the rebound to swipe upward this time.

A dull shock ran through my arms, and the sword rebounded sideways.

Eugeo hadn't faltered from the pain of being sliced from shoulder to chest for even an instant. He'd used his right leg's greave to smack my sword out of the way. Realizing that this action also put him in position for a counterattack, I felt a wave of horror run down my back and twisted desperately. The Blue Rose Sword came roaring toward me from the left.

I barely avoided a blow to the neck but couldn't get all the way clear. He cut a line across my left shoulder. Rather than pain, I felt a searing chill there and launched myself off my right foot to throw my wounded shoulder at Eugeo for a body blow.

This time, I *did* feel a blinding pain, and blood spurted into the air. Through the red mist, I saw Eugeo steadying himself on his left leg to keep from falling.

A direct counter would be impossible from that position. I held my sword to the right, one-handed once again. The black surface of the sword shone pale blue—this would be the diagonal-slash attack Slant. If I hit him on the right shoulder, he'd be wounded on both sides and unable to swing the same way again.

"Raaaah!"

But right as I was about to unleash this attack, a surge of red light shot out from the far side of Eugeo's body.

It was the light of a sword skill. But there was no Aincrad skill that would allow him to attack from a position with his right rear side exposed to me.

Both stunned and unable to stop the momentum at this point, I activated the Slant. A moment later, Eugeo's body spun counterclockwise at ferocious speed. A bright-red slash shot toward me from the left.

I recognized it as the two-handed skill Backlash—a counterattack skill that worked against a foe standing behind you. But I had never taught it to Eugeo.

The resulting impact completely jarred these thoughts out of my mind. My Slant and Eugeo's Backlash collided, and our swords rebounded hard. As fresh blood streamed from our shoulders, Eugeo and I found ourselves readying our swords straight overhead in perfect synchronization.

Two blades shining a deep blue for the single downward strike Vertical.

While it was classified as a vertical strike, the trajectory was not necessarily set in stone. It was common for the angle to tilt as much as ten degrees, according to the position of the dominant hand. Thus, it was possible for two people facing each other to have paths that would intersect and force each of them backward.

It started out that way this time, too. The black and Blue Rose swords met at about a third of the length from their tips, throwing off blinding sparks.

But unlike in the old *SAO*, there were times in the Underworld when two sword skills would meet and not deflect each other. I suspected it was when the fierce will to battle—the strength of mental image, or Incarnation—on the part of both combatants acted as a brake on the system's natural tendency to repel the weapons.

The swords were locked together, spraying orange sparks and flashing blue light. In this third stalemate, Eugeo and I were thrust face-to-face, our arms and swords locked in total equilibrium as we each tried to follow through and finish the skill.

I stared into Eugeo's pupils beyond the showering sparks and, through clenched teeth, hissed, "…Does that attack of yours have a name?"

With a face as still as a frozen pond, Eugeo replied, "…Baltio style, Storm Wave."

Off the top of my head, I couldn't remember where I'd heard that style's name before. I frowned, and then it came to me.

Baltio style. It was the school of swordsmanship practiced by elite disciple Golgorosso Balto, the mentor under whom Eugeo had served as page at the North Centoria Imperial Swordcraft Academy until this March.

Because it was plain and unadorned in comparison to the Nor-kia and High-Norkia styles, the higher noble students looked down on it, as they did to the Serlut style used by Sortiliena, who was my own tutor.

But in fact, this was just a sign that it was a more practical style. And for the year that he'd been a page, Eugeo had received a thorough education in its ways, courtesy of Golgorosso. And that gave rise to another mystery.

"Eugeo…do you remember the person who taught you that move?" I asked again, putting every last ounce of strength into the intersection of our blades. A moment later, I got the answer I expected:

"I don't remember, and I don't care."

He must've been putting just as much of his power into the stalemate as I was, but his voice and expression were utterly cold and dry.

"I only need to know about *her*," he continued. "She is the reason I use my sword. My existence is dedicated to eliminating her enemies…"

"…"

So he'd forgotten not only Alice and me but Golgorosso as well. And yet he knew the names of his skills and how to execute them. Completely resetting the memories of the person being made an Integrity Knight meant that they would lose all that accumulated training and all those learned sacred arts. It was why Administrator had come up with the complicated work-around that was the Synthesis Ritual.

Rather than deleting all of the target's memories, it blocked their access, making it impossible to recall what was still there. I didn't know the precise logic behind it, but it seemed similar to what we would call retrograde amnesia in the real world: loss of memories of oneself and others, but language and life skills preserved.

The thing blocking the proper flow of Eugeo's memories was the Piety Module that was placed inside his soul, his fluctlight.

But whose memories were in the space where the module sat now? If I knew that, it would be the first step to getting him to come to his senses…

But no.

I would need more than just words to break that woman's wicked spell. I'd traded sword blows with so many people since the very first day I was locked inside the world of Aincrad—Asuna, Suguha, Sinon, Yuuki. And in this world, there had been Sortiliena, first-seat disciple Volo, and knights like Eldrie, Deusolbert, and Fanatio. Even Alice, who was watching this fight from just a short distance away.

Swords in the virtual world weren't just polygonal bits of data. Because our lives were resting on them, the feelings that we imbued the blades with could reach the soul of our opponents. I chose to believe that a sword freed from hatred could sometimes foster an understanding that surpassed mere words.

The blue light of Vertical slowly began to fade from our deadlocked swords. I wrung out every last drop of power from my body.

I had to make sure that the entirety of my being was reaching out toward my friend's soul.

"Eugeooooo!!" I shouted the moment the sword skill ended, pulling back my sword.

I struck with all my might. My attack was blocked. Eugeo slashed. I met his strike at the base of the blade. Our feet stayed in place, where we could keep swinging with the shortest possible range. A steady stream of clashes and sparks flew, filling the room with sound and light.

"Rrraaaaahhh!!" I bellowed.

"Seyyyaaaaah!!" Eugeo added, his first roar of the fight.

Faster. Faster!

I strung together a continuous line of attacks—no skills or form or strategy, just pure instinct—and Eugeo kept up perfectly. With each trade of blows, I sensed the invisible shell around him cracking.

Eventually I realized that I had a fierce grin on my lips. I recalled that there was a time long ago that Eugeo and I had fought wildly like this, a good liberating sword brawl. It wasn't in the training hall at the academy. Not along the journey to Centoria. No, it was in the fields and forests close to Rulid…We pretended we were practicing with our swords, using wooden blades that were practically toys…whacking one another like rambunctious little boys…

But did Eugeo and I really do that, right after we met in the woods two years ago?

Were those cracks actually…in *my* memory……?

Ka-chiiiing! A sharper metallic clang broke my momentary trance. The black sword and the Blue Rose Sword met at the perfect angle again, canceling out each other's momentum, falling still where they crossed.

"…Eugeo…?" I whispered.

I saw his lips move in response.

I didn't hear his voice, but I could tell that the knight in silver and blue had murmured my name.

His normally smooth, pale forehead was now creased and jagged. I could see teeth clenched shut through his parted lips and a weak flicker of light in his cold, dark eyes. They looked over my shoulder at Alice, who was hanging back along the wall.

His lips trembled again, forming Alice's name with no voice behind them.

"Eugeo…Do you remember, Eugeo?!" I called out. That caused my blade to slip. It was unable to withstand the full pressure of the Blue Rose Sword and faltered backward.

I lost my balance and had to struggle to stay on my feet. I knew I was a sitting duck—but Eugeo did nothing to follow up. He just stood there, holding his sword out at an odd angle.

I retreated and came to a stop near Alice, sucked in a deep breath, and expelled all of it at once.

"Eugeooooo!!"

He flinched, and his downcast face slowly rose.

It was as pale as ever, but this time there was true expression upon it. Confusion, anxiety, regret, and affection...All these emotions that had been frozen by the ritual combined into one faint smile that seemed to shake the shell of thick ice that surrounded him, just a bit.

"...Kirito," he said, and a moment later, "Alice..."

I heard it clearly this time. Eugeo spoke our names out loud.

It had worked. My sword...reached him...crossing the boundaries that separated his heart from mine.

"Eugeo..."

The thin smile that rested on his lips deepened. He spun the Blue Rose Sword around in his hand to hold it in a reverse grip. His arm lowered until the tip of the sword landed on the marble floor. It crackled, and the slightly misty weapon sank in about an inch.

I saw that as a sign that the battle was over, and I lowered my sword. The breath I'd been holding escaped, and I took a step forward with my right leg.

But the next moment was just the start of a series of events I failed to predict.

"Kirito!"

That was Alice, calling me over my shoulder. I hadn't sensed her coming; her left arm circled around my torso and lifted me up straight.

Then more words escaped from Eugeo's lips.

"...Release Recollection."

That was the phrase. The initiation of the greatest of battle abilities in the Underworld, calling forth the memory of the weapon and unlocking the true heart of superpowered Perfect Weapon Control—the secret of Memory Release.

Bright blue-white light shot from his sword.

I couldn't dodge or defend against it. Absolute cold spread from the blade, instantly freezing the entirety of the vast chamber. The mouth of the descending staircase in the corner of the room, the levitating disc that went up to the top floor, and both Alice and I were frozen solid up to our chests in thick, immobilizing ice. If Alice hadn't straightened me up, the ice would have swallowed my head.

When we came across Bercouli Synthesis One in the great bath on the ninety-fifth floor of the cathedral, he had been frozen up to his neck like this. Eugeo's Memory Release power was strong enough to freeze an entire pool of hot bathwater so fast that even the oldest of the knights wasn't able to escape. I hadn't forgotten or overlooked that, but there wasn't even any water to freeze on this floor. And he hadn't generated a huge number of ice elements to make use of—where had all this ice come from?

But even that wasn't the shocking part.

Why did Eugeo do it? He just got his memory back; why would he need to lock me and Alice in ice?

Against the all-consuming, piercing chill, I just barely had the strength to make my mouth form the words "Eugeo...why......?"

About fifty feet away, Eugeo got back to his feet easily and favored me with a sad little smile. "I'm sorry, Kirito...and Alice. Please don't come after me..."

And then my best friend, and Alice's childhood companion, pulled the Blue Rose Sword from the floor and headed for the levitating disc in the center of the chamber.

The large marble platform, like the staircase and us, was covered in thick ice, but the knight simply walked over it and jabbed the end of the sword down lightly. It began to rise, ice shards cracking and sprinkling off.

As the disc ascended, I saw that smile stay on Eugeo's face, an expression attempting to withstand a whole host of conflicting emotions, until he eventually vanished through the hole above.

"...Eu...ge...oooooo!!" I screamed, but it was drowned out by the hard, heavy sound of the disc fitting seamlessly back into the ceiling.

2

"Remove Core Protection."

Just three command words, a phrase he'd never heard before in his life. But the moment that he finished repeating them, Eugeo came to realize that he'd just unlocked a door that was never meant to be opened.

Just one hour before that unthinkable duel against Kirito, Eugeo had barely managed a painful draw against Bercouli, commander of the Integrity Knights and wielder of a blade that cut into the future. By utilizing the Memory Release feature of the Blue Rose Sword, he had been able to freeze them both in place, until a strange man named Prime Senator Chudelkin had taken his unconscious body up to the hundredth floor of Central Cathedral.

It was there that Eugeo had met a girl with silver hair and mirror eyes, the otherworldly beauty that was Administrator, pontifex of the Church. Through a mental haze that refused to lift, he'd listened to her speak.

You are a flower in its flower bed, deprived of the water that is love.

But I am different. I will love you, and only you.

However, only if you love me just the same.

It was like they were sacred arts commands in and of themselves, binding his will to them. He'd felt himself repeating the three command words as she'd bidden him.

It must've been some kind of forbidden art. Something that hurled open the door meant to protect truly precious things—memories, thoughts...the soul.

With that perfect smile, Administrator had peered into Eugeo's mind, looked around, and inserted something deep inside it, something colder than ice.

Then he'd lost consciousness again.

When he awoke, it was as though he were being dredged up from the bottom of a deep, dark blackness, answering someone's distant call.

Bright sparks. Silver steel. And a young man with black hair, furiously fighting against him.

That was when Eugeo recognized that he was clad in the armor of an Integrity Knight and that he was using his sword on the friend he trusted more than anyone in the world and the childhood sweetheart he'd cared for more than any other soul.

But even that realization did not remove the icy thorn jabbing into the center of his mind. It bound his thoughts to its will, ceaselessly ordering him to strike down these foes for the glory of the supreme Administrator. Helpless to stop himself, Eugeo activated the Blue Rose Sword's Memory Release art, locking those two precious souls in ice. He resisted in vain, but it was the only way to stop the fight.

...I gave in to her temptations and destroyed something that should never have been destroyed. But even still, there are things I can do...things I must do.

"...I'm sorry, Kirito...and Alice," he managed to say.

Eugeo stepped onto the levitating platform to return to the hundredth floor of the tower—to Administrator's bedchamber.

When it came to a heavy stop, the moonlight coming through the enormous windows reflected off Eugeo's armor and sword, sending sheets of pale light through the room.

It was about two o'clock in the morning on the twenty-fifth day of the fifth month of the year.

Just three days ago, at this hour of the night he was in his bed in the elite disciples' dorm. He always slept like a rock after a full day of lessons and training and never awoke before the morning bell.

Thinking back on the last few nights, he remembered that he'd spent the twenty-second in the school's detention cell and the twenty-third in the underground jail beneath the Axiom Church's grounds—hardly the best conditions for sleep. After the early-morning escape on the twenty-fourth, he'd been through battle after battle, a thought that made his body go numb with the weight of fatigue, but that pulsing, throbbing thorn of ice stuck in his head kept him from being sleepy.

Give your everything to the pontifex. Fight to protect the Axiom Church, the thorn commanded, both as stern as a steel whip and as sweet as the finest honey. In reality, the "thorn" was probably the same purple crystal that had been stuck in Eldrie's forehead. And Eugeo got the feeling that if he gave in and tasted that honey again, his mind would never return.

The only reason he had any consciousness at the moment was because of Kirito's desperate appeal and the ferocity of their swordfight. And the reason he could return largely unharmed was thanks to Alice watching them fight, rather than getting involved.

Alice Synthesis Thirty's skill with the sword and the Perfect Weapon Control version of her Osmanthus Blade, a storm of golden petals, was a combination far beyond Eugeo's current ability to counteract. If she had drawn her weapon and fought alongside Kirito, Eugeo would have fallen before he could have ever regained his own mind.

He didn't know exactly why Alice would have pledged herself to rebellion against the Axiom Church. Perhaps, as he imagined while ascending the staircase, Kirito had managed to convince her. Perhaps it was something even more impressive than that.

There had been a bandage over Alice's right eye that appeared to be fashioned from Kirito's ripped clothing. Eugeo guessed that whatever had happened had been the same as when Eugeo himself had attacked Humbert Zizek at the academy. Her right eye must have exploded when she committed the crime of declaring war against the Church. Both the first time they'd seen her at the academy and later in the Cloudtop Garden of the eightieth floor, they'd been totally unable to stop Alice. And it wasn't Eugeo who had brought her to that momentous decision, but Kirito…

But I don't have the right to complain about that now. I gave in to Administrator's honeyed words. I cast open the door to my heart. It was a betrayal of Kirito and Alice. Of Tiese, and Ronie, and Frenica, and Golgorosso and Sortiliena, and Miss Azurica the dorm manager, and Sadore the craftsman, and everyone on Walde Farm, and Selka and Old Man Garitta back in Rulid, and Elder Gasfut, and the little sage Cardinal in her hidden library.

He clenched the pommel of his sword, withstanding the chilling throb as it steadily grew worse. There wouldn't be much time left for him to maintain his wits like this. He had to atone for his sins before he vanished for good.

There was only one way to do that.

Eugeo raised his head and looked around. The placement of the ninety-ninth and hundredth floors had to be unbalanced, as the disc had put him on the south side of the room here. The only thing beyond the glass windows that surrounded the room was a full blanket of stars. The massive sword decorations on the pillars between the windowpanes gleamed with the light of the moon and stars.

Suddenly, he got the sense that someone had called for him, and he looked up.

The pure-white domed ceiling over ten mels above featured a mural, which he'd seen the first time he'd come here, of the story of the gods. Among the gods and dragons and human beings in the image were embedded tiny crystals that shone with their own light.

…Is it that light that's calling me…?

He squinted, focusing on one of the crystals. Then he heard an *actual* voice from a different direction and hastily looked forward.

In the middle of the vast chamber was a circular bed that had to be ten whole mels across. The drapes were down around the sides, blocking the interior from view. But if he focused, he could hear a faint voice on the other side of the sheer material. A voice that sang as much as it whispered, threaded with sweet, dulcet tones.

The voice of Administrator.

It sounded like she was chanting a sacred art, but it didn't have the fierce rigor of an attack spell. If she was performing some typical, everyday kind of housekeeping art, now was his chance.

He put the Blue Rose Sword in its sheath and laid it on the floor, then removed the armor that had been damaged in the fight with Kirito. Off went the gauntlets, the boots, and the cape, until he was dressed in his usual shirt and trousers. Eugeo brushed at his chest with his fingers, just to make sure that what he needed was still there.

He took one step toward the canopy, then another.

A squat figure tottered closer from farther within the bed. It produced an unpleasant chortle.

"Hoh-hee, hwee-hee-hee…I figured buying me a good five or ten minutes would be about right. I didn't actually expect you to come back *alive*. Perhaps you're a better find than I realized!"

The instant he saw the figure in the moonlight, Eugeo's breath caught in his throat. It was all he could do not to grimace.

He wore hideous clothes, bright red on the right half and bright blue on the left. The middle of his balloon-like chest was an ugly patchwork. His face was pale white, with narrow eyes like slits in his face and a long, upturned mouth. The gold cap he wore atop his bald pate was gone, but Eugeo would never mistake the remaining features as belonging to anyone else.

This was Prime Senator Chudelkin. He had shown up at the end of Eugeo and Bercouli's fight, cast a Deep Freeze art that had turned the commander to stone, and then transported the unconscious Eugeo up here to the top floor.

While he looked just like a short, silly clown, he was almost certainly the most powerful sacred arts user after the pontifex herself, and a cruel inquisitor in the extreme. If he found out that Eugeo was (temporarily) back in his right mind, he would use that petrification art without missing a beat. The only way Eugeo could fulfill his final duty was if he managed to get past this man without suspicion.

Chudelkin cast a glance at the armor Eugeo had set on the floor, and his nearly hairless eyebrows shot upward theatrically.

"Oh, my, you certainly did a number on the armor that Her Holiness gave to you. I sincerely hope you did not receive this beating from those brazen rebels and come running back with your tail between your legs, Number Thirty-Two...?"

Her Holiness had to be Administrator, *those brazen rebels* would be Kirito and Alice, and *Number Thirty-Two* was his own designation as an Integrity Knight. He felt like he'd give away the game no matter what he said, but he had to answer the question one way or another.

Eugeo steeled himself and kept his face as devoid of emotion as he could. "I locked the two rebels in ice, Prime Senator."

Chudelkin's eyes curved as though he were beaming with all his might, but the pupils themselves glittered with cold, hard malice. "Hoh-hoh. You locked them in ice...? All very well, all very good...but you *did* finish the job, didn't you, Number Thirty-Two?"

"..."

Throughout that moment of silence, Eugeo's mind raced.

Of course he hadn't killed either Kirito or Alice. The Blue Rose Sword's advanced ability was designed only to imprison its targets, not to harm them. As long as their faces were exposed, they wouldn't lose much life despite being stuck under thick ice.

Would it be better to not mention that and to just say they were done for? If Chudelkin went down below and saw for himself, he'd uncover that lie in short time. This was the sort of situation where Kirito would use his intuition and courage to come up with the perfect answer on the spot.

All I ever did was hide behind him. Whenever there was trouble, I looked to my partner for help. Every big decision was his to make.

This time, I have to think, and I have to decide. Kirito didn't just leave all of the big calls up to his gut. He thought his hardest, picked out the right answer, and got me all the way here.

I have to think like he would.

Eugeo thought so hard that for a moment, he actually forgot about the cold throbbing in the center of his head. His lips parted, and he spoke with the absolute minimum of volume.

"No, I did not finish them off, Prime Senator. The pontifex ordered me to 'stop' the rebels."

He didn't actually know whether that was the order he'd been given by Administrator. But from what he could vaguely remember, the first time he had awakened in this chamber, the man had not been there. If Chudelkin hadn't been around when Eugeo was turned into an Integrity Knight, he couldn't judge the content of any orders—and if Administrator had said it, this man couldn't possibly override that.

Of course, if Administrator herself was listening from the bed just ten mels away, then all was lost. But she seemed to be in the midst of chanting some kind of sacred art through the layers of hanging canopy. There was a good chance that as long as they whispered, she wouldn't hear.

Eugeo waited for Chudelkin's response, desperately controlling his expression to keep his nerves from showing. The little clown man's huge lips twisted, and he scowled.

"Very poor, Number Thirty-Two, very poor indeed!"

He jabbed a finger at Eugeo's face. "When you refer to me, you must call me 'Lord Prime Senator.' Understand that? *Lord!* The next time that you forget that, you'll be my steed! I'll ride around on your back, digging my heels into your sides—hi-hoh, hi-hoh! Hwe-hee-hee-hee!"

He cackled in falsetto, then clasped his hands over his mouth and peered toward the bed. Once he was sure that Administrator's sacred art was continuing without interruption, he made a grand gesture of calming himself down, then beamed.

"...Well, I ought to carry out Her Holiness's orders for *me* now. That miserable, corrupted knight must be put in Deep Freeze at once. Oh, and you'll wait right here, Number Thirty-Two. It's no fun if others are around to interfere, you see. Hoh, hoh-hoh-hoh."

Eugeo nodded, stifling the sickening lurch rising in his chest.

Chudelkin tottered over to the levitating platform on the south end of the room. Like he did to Commander Bercouli, he likely had all kinds of humiliating treatment in mind for Kirito and Alice while they were stone.

But there shouldn't have been any concern for them. The prison of ice the Blue Rose Sword created was nothing compared to Alice's Perfect Weapon Control. In the Cloudtop Garden, Eugeo had locked Alice's entire body in ice. But the Osmanthus Blade had turned into countless tiny shards that had carved the ice into nothing.

Either they were already out of the ice by now, or Alice would use that merciless power of hers as soon as Chudelkin showed up. For his part, the fat little man hopped onto the platform, huffing and wheezing, and headed downward. Eugeo watched and waited as the platform returned empty, fusing into the floor like always. The prime senator must have let the platform go back up so that he could enjoy himself in peace. It left no way to know what was happening on the ninety-ninth floor.

It's all right. The stupid man can't beat them.

Eugeo took a deep breath to steady his nerves and returned his gaze to the center of the room. He lifted his left hand and pressed down on the shirt over his chest.

I just have to fulfill my role.

He steeled his resolve, picked up the sword, and started walking forward. He was just three mels away from the bed, then two, then one.

Just then, the endlessly droning sacred arts chanting came to an abrupt stop, like it had been snuffed out. Eugeo automatically froze, mind racing.

Did the sacred art just happen to finish right then, or did she stop because she sensed him approaching? What kind of spell was it, anyway?

His head swiveled around, but nothing seemed different. The circular room was larger than the floor below, perhaps forty mels across, and there was hardly any furniture inside—just the bed, the thick carpet, and more than a dozen pillars with massive sword decorations to serve as frames for the windows that surrounded the room. They had gleamed golden in the moonlight, but nothing seemed different about them now.

Eugeo gave up on his examination and faced the bed again. Instantly, the middle of his head throbbed.

The cold pain was getting stronger, bit by bit. He probably wouldn't be lucid for much longer. Before he became an Integrity Knight in body and mind again, he would do what needed to be done.

He took a few more steps, right up to the side of the bed, and after some hesitation, laid the Blue Rose Sword on the ground. The instant he let go, he felt anxiety and loneliness, but he had to remove any reason for the woman to suspect him of being a threat.

Eugeo straightened up, took a deep breath, and prayed that his voice wouldn't tremble.

"...My lady Pontifex."

After a few seconds of silence, which felt eminently longer, her voice replied.

"...Welcome back, Eugeo. You finished your errand properly."

"...Yes, my lady," he muttered. Eugeo was bad at acting, but he'd spent years of his life in Rulid suppressing his emotions. All he had to do was go back to that time in his life. Back to the old him, before he met that strange, black-haired boy at the Gigas Cedar.

"Very good. Then I owe you a reward. Come into my bed," came the soft, velvety welcome beyond the canopy.

He brushed the front of his chest again, then gently pulled open the part in the canopy surrounding the bed. It was all purple darkness inside, but the sweet, familiar scent there lured him in deeper.

He put his weight on the silk cover and crawled forward. While it might have been voluminous for a bed, it was still supposed to be only five mels to the center. Yet no matter how many crawling repetitions he did, he couldn't see or feel anything ahead.

But if he panicked or said something, it would tell her that his mind was back under his own control. He kept moving, focusing only on the feel of the covers.

Suddenly, a bit higher than his eye level, a pale light appeared without a sound.

That color wasn't coming from a candle or a lamp. It was a light element from a sacred art, though he never heard any commands. The floating little mote peeled back the velvet darkness just the tiniest bit.

Eugeo looked down and saw *her* smiling face, just two mels away. For an instant, his eyes bulged, but then he composed his face again just as quickly and bowed with his hands still pressed against the bed.

It was a girl dressed in sheer purple fabric, with long silvery hair. The ruler of humanity, with transcendent beauty and mirror eyes that kept her thoughts hidden.

Administrator, pontifex of the Axiom Church.

The young woman seated lazily on the blanket stared at Eugeo, silver mirror eyes reflecting the light of the little floating element, and whispered, "Come to me, Eugeo. As I promised, I will give you what you want. The love that belongs only to you."

".........Yes, my lady," he whispered, inching closer to her, still prone.

Once he was one mel away, he'd leap on her, cover her mouth with his hand so she couldn't give commands, pull his secret weapon out from under his shirt with the other hand, and stab her with it. It would take less than two seconds altogether, but that still seemed like an eternity against someone like Administrator.

The instant he thought of this act of rebellion against her, a sharp pain ran from the spot between his eyebrows to the center of his head. But there was no time to think about it. He had to relax as much as he could and sneak closer, closer…

"But before that," Administrator murmured just before he reached the right distance, causing him to pause, "I want you to show me your face again, Eugeo."

Did she sense his malice? If he tried to execute his plan now, he wouldn't be in time. He had to obey.

Slowly he rose off the sheets and looked at her, keeping his expression frozen. At the very least, he wanted to keep from looking into her eyes, but those glassy surfaces drew his gaze through some irresistible force. They betrayed no information of their own and yet had the ability to peer directly into the mind of any who looked into them. The floating light caused them to reflect an eerie glint.

After several interminable seconds, the woman said, "Conveniently, there was a hole in your memory already, so I inserted the module right there. Perhaps I shouldn't have been so lazy…"

It seemed like she was mostly talking to herself, and Eugeo didn't understand at first.

There was a hole in his memory—meaning that something had been missing from Eugeo's memory even before he was first taken to this chamber? But he had no inkling that there was some missing period of his life before this. Maybe the fact that he didn't remember it *was* the hole in his memory, but there had been that thing Cardinal said, too.

To insert the Piety Module, the most precious memories of the target had to be removed first, usually of their most beloved person.

That conversation in the hidden library seemed like it was ages ago by now. Eugeo mulled this over.

*   *   *

...My most beloved person. That would be Alice Zuberg, the girl who was taken away by an Integrity Knight before my eyes eight years ago. I've never once forgotten her. When I close my eyes, I can see her golden hair shining in the sun, her eyes bluer than the bluest midsummer sky, and that dazzling smile.

...And while it might not be the same kind of love, I also have a partner, a friend almost as important to me as Alice. A strange young man I met in the forest south of Rulid two years and two months ago. A "Lost Child of Vecta," with black hair and black eyes in the eastern style. Kirito's been my best friend—he got me out of the village and helped guide me all the way here to Central Cathedral. I can easily see that mischievous grin of his, too.

...Alice and Kirito. I may never see their smiles again. But even if I'm fated to lose my life here, I know that up to that final moment, I'll never forget about them.

...I was hoping I'd be able to go back to Rulid with Kirito and Alice once she got her memory back...but I don't have the right to wish for that anymore. I gave in to Administrator's temptation. I lost sight of myself. I turned my sword on the two people I care about most.

Just as he reached that conclusion, Eugeo felt his eye twitch just the tiniest bit. Administrator tilted her head in slight confusion, though it was unclear how she chose to interpret that motion.

"Yes, you seem a bit unstable still. Very well, I'll just have to resynthesize. Your reward can come after that, Eugeo."

She thrust out her right hand.

It might have been the perfect moment to leap into action, but the moment that her delicate finger pointed at his forehead, Eugeo underwent a most peculiar sensation. His body jolted and went numb, leaving him unable to even speak, much less move his limbs.

And the next instant, a very bizarre feeling shot from the spot between his eyes toward the back of his head.

The source of the cold throbbing, that thorn of ice jabbing deep into his head, was being slowly but forcefully pulled out from its location. It didn't hurt, but each movement of the thorn brought a bright flash to his eyes, and brief glimpses of vague scenes.

Green branches swaying in the wind. Gently shifting sunlight coming through the trees.

Running and laughing beneath them.

Shining golden hair just ahead.

Coarse black hair bouncing right beside.

Young Eugeo looked to his right as he ran. But the smile of his other childhood friend drifted away into a bright flash, out of reach…

A powerful shock brought Eugeo back to the surface of the bed in the darkness. As his numb body arched its back, something alien was protruding from his forehead. A triangular, translucent prism that glowed purple.

When they'd fought Eldrie the Integrity Knight in the rose garden, the mention of his mother's name had caused him to act strangely, until this same kind of prism emerged from his head. But the one appearing out of Eugeo right now was larger, carved with more-intricate symbols, and glowing brighter.

Stunned with both the shock that something this enormous had been inside his head all this time and the horror that Administrator's sacred arts were powerful enough to do such a thing, Eugeo could only watch in silence.

"Yes…be a good boy. Just stay there," the silver-haired young woman purred. She reached out and gently plucked the purple prism from Eugeo's head. The moment the object came loose, his mind went blank, and Eugeo slumped helplessly into the linens.

Administrator cradled the prism in her fingertips, gazing upon it lovingly. "This is an improved model of the module. I just finished making it. Not only does it force loyalty to me and the Church, it also contains circuits for strengthening the imagination. Synthesize this, and there won't be any need for inefficient training. You'll be able to use Incarnation that very instant. It's still limited to very elementary steps for now, however…"

Eugeo understood less than half of what she was saying. But one thing was clear—that prism, the Piety Module, was what took over his thoughts, turned him into an Integrity Knight, and made him threaten his friends. Yes, he had chosen that path for himself, but now that the module was removed, he could fulfill his final role without that bothersome false obedience getting in the way. Now he realized that the horribly cold, stinging pain in the center of his head was gone, too.

However, even with the module gone, the numbness that came over him when she pointed her finger at him did not go away. He was completely unable to control his own limbs.

If only he could move his right hand. Then he could grab the thing from his chest and swing it down on her...

He struggled with all his might, stuck with his back hunched over—and then her hand was reaching out again.

Eugeo rolled his eyes upward and saw the pontifex, module in her left hand, approaching close enough that their knees were nearly touching. Unable to resist even the slightest of pressures, his head was pulled toward the smiling woman, and he toppled forward.

Administrator rested his head sideways on her lap and traced his hairline with her fingertip. "Show me your memories again. This time, I'll bury this in the most precious place of all. Then your head won't hurt anymore. Even better...you'll be forever free of all those pointless, petty troubles and pains, your hunger and thirst."

The pale finger pulled away, then descended to brush his lips. The numbing feeling went away but only around his mouth.

She removed her hand again, gave him a mind-melting smile, and commanded, "Now say those words I taught you, one more time."

" ... "

Now that they were barely under his control again, Eugeo's lips trembled. His memory of fighting with Kirito as an Integrity Knight was fuzzy, as was whatever came before that, but he did have a very clear picture of the three command words he had chanted.

Remove Core Protection.

The sacred words were unfamiliar to him, and he couldn't guess what they signified, but one thing was certain: That short command was designed to seize the door that all people were born with—a door that stayed shut to keep the mind safe—and hurl it open.

That was how Administrator had been able to peer into Eugeo's memory and find the empty space into which she inserted the Piety Module. But according to her words, the synthesis process had been unstable, which was why she was trying to do the same thing again.

Despite the incredible danger he was in, Eugeo was still in his right mind, which meant the door was shut again. Either it closed on its own over time, or the pontifex had closed it afterward for some reason or another; he couldn't be sure. Whatever the case, in order to resynthesize him, Administrator required that Eugeo utter the three-word command again.

If he did, he would almost certainly become an Integrity Knight in every sense and would never again get the chance to restore Alice's memory.

But if he didn't say them, Administrator would detect his rebellion against her.

This was the moment. Right here, with her skin exposed and defenseless, Eugeo had his last and best chance. He had to find a way to restore feeling to his numbed hands and stab her.

With just a gesture of her hands, she had paralyzed his body. And not just that—she'd also generated that light element above without uttering a word.

There was another occasion on which Eugeo had witnessed an invisible power being used without a spoken command, although it was not the same kind of sacred art. It was Bercouli Synthesis One, whom he'd fought in the bathhouse many floors below—though Eugeo originally knew him as the ancient hero who had founded the village of Rulid. With just a motion of his hand, he had drawn his distant sword to his side.

In fact, that wasn't the only time. In the Great Library, Cardinal had closed off passages with a wave of her staff and made a table appear out of nowhere. There must be a level of power at which simple thoughts could have the same effect as the chanting of sacred arts.

Of course, Eugeo had been a simple student at the academy just days ago. His ability with sacred arts wasn't even as good as the apprentices in the Axiom Church, much less masters like Administrator and Cardinal.

But at this moment—right now—he had to break this paralysis with nothing but the power of his mind.

Kirito once told him that what was most important in this world was what you put into your sword. In other words, the sword would take on the power that came from your heart and mind, making its bite sharper and stronger.

If your mind could make your sword stronger, then the same thing could be true of sacred arts...or of anything and everything that human beings did.

Move, Eugeo prayed, opening his lips and breathing steadily. *Move, hand, move.*

I've made so many mistakes in my life. I failed to save Alice when the Integrity Knight took her away. I spent years not going after her. Right when I was finally at the end of that long journey, I lost sight of my goal. I have to make up for all that weakness.

"...M—..."

A hoarse sound escaped from his throat.

"...Mo—..."

Administrator's smile, just above his head, waned. Her silver mirrors narrowed, searching for Eugeo's intention. There was no turning back now. He focused all the energy he could summon into his right hand.

But the numbness was not abating. Countless invisible needles stabbed at his fingers and palm, keeping them trapped in place. If only he could just move his hand this one moment, it could shatter into pieces afterward. He didn't need to swing a sword again. Just one little…

"…Mo—ve…," he uttered, wringing out the sounds.

Just then, light enveloped the hand that was resting on the bedsheet. It was warm and gentle and seemed to melt all the pain away. Instantly, the icy thorns that gouged his flesh and bones disappeared.

"…What are you…?" Administrator murmured and tried to pull away. But Eugeo's mobile hand was already sneaking into the collar of his shirt and grabbing the object that was hanging on the chain around his neck.

It was a tiny dagger that gleamed deep bronze.

He pulled it out and jabbed it downward, toward the white skin visible above the deep collar of Administrator's sheer nightgown.

It was impossible to miss. The blade of the weapon was barely five cens long, but they were basically touching already—there was no way he would come up short.

But just as that needlelike tip was about to pierce the skin of Administrator's body, something happened that beggared belief.

Craaak!! There was a blast like thunder, and a film of purple light appeared, centered around the point of the dagger. The glowing surface was made up of strings of extremely tiny sacred script. They were so small they shouldn't have had any mass at all, but the thin film was resisting the sharp tip of the weapon.

"Hrrggh…!!"

Eugeo gritted his teeth and summoned all his willpower, trying to break through the resistance. Cardinal had given him and Kirito one of these daggers each. It had almost no attack power of its own, but whatever target he used it on would be vulnerable to the remote sacred arts of the little sage in her isolated library.

Eugeo's dagger was supposed to put Alice the Integrity Knight to sleep, and Kirito's was supposed to defeat Administrator. But he had already used his own to save the life of Fanatio Synthesis

Two, the vice commander of the knights, whom they had fought on the fiftieth floor.

At the time, Cardinal's bodiless voice had told them, "There is a high likelihood that Administrator is not in a waking state at the moment. If you can reach the top floor before she wakes, you can eliminate her without needing the dagger."

But they hadn't been in time. Now that she was awake, the only way to beat Administrator, who had just as much power as Cardinal, was to use the dagger in Eugeo's hand.

He'd wanted to return Alice's memories and take her back to Rulid with him. It had been his only desire for years. But then he'd allowed himself to fall under the pontifex's sway, even temporarily, put on the Integrity Knight armor, and threatened both Kirito *and* Alice with his sword. Eugeo could sense that his original wish would never come true. It couldn't.

But if there was some way he could atone for his sin, it would be to abandon himself—to carry out this act not for his own personal conviction but in service of a much larger destiny.

Eleven-year-old Alice, taken from her hometown, bereft of her memories, and turned into a knight.

Tiese and Ronie, perfectly innocent girls, violated over nothing more than noble birthright.

These were the products of a warped, corrupt system of rule, and he would use the last remnants of his strength and life to destroy that. If he had to die in order to ensure that the pontifex fell, then all the time he spent on his journey and at the academy would have had a purpose after all.

But despite all that resolution, that determination, the thin purple film was keeping him from Administrator's skin. Meanwhile, she clearly hadn't predicted Eugeo's actions, as she was arching her back away from him and breathing heavily.

There was rage in those gaping mirror eyes now. Eugeo added his left hand to his right, trying with all his strength to push the dagger through.

"Yaaaaah!"

The needlelike point pierced barely a single milice into the shining protective layer—and then the sacred writing that formed the barrier exploded into bright light, blasting Eugeo and Administrator backward.

"...!!"

He tumbled through the air as though slapped by an invisible giant's palm, but even as it knocked him completely off the bed, Eugeo was able to achieve two things simultaneously.

He got a fresh grip on the chain holding the dagger before it could fall out of his grasp, and the moment that his back hit the floor, he reached out with his other hand to grab the sheath of the Blue Rose Sword, which was right next to him.

Even with the heavy sword weighing him down, his backward momentum continued, rolling him along the floor until at last his back smashed against one of the giant windows that separated the room from the world without.

"Nng..."

Wincing against the pain, Eugeo raised his head and looked to the center of the room.

The hanging canopy sheets around the bed had all been blown clean away, exposing the circular bed. On the far side of it stood a silent figure. Like Eugeo, she'd been blasted backward by the explosion of the barrier, but the only damage she seemed to have received was the swaying of her long hair. In her left hand was the shining prism she'd taken out of his head.

The sheer purple cloth she'd been wearing hadn't withstood the impact, however. But Administrator didn't show the slightest bit of concern about her nakedness. She reached up with her free hand to smooth out her long silver hair.

Then she sat from a standing position, as though there were an invisible chair behind her, and crossed her slender legs. She moved silently through the air, not breaking her posture, until she stopped about ten mels away from where Eugeo lay prone on the south edge of the room.

From atop her invisible throne, the pontifex placed her fingers against her chin and stared at Eugeo. He was unable to move or speak. Eventually the silver-eyed young woman grinned and said, "I was just wondering where you hid that tool of yours…I suppose it was the doing of the little one in the library, wasn't it? She filtered it out of my senses. In the time since I've seen her last, she's gotten rather crafty, hasn't she?"

She chuckled deep in her throat. "But too bad. I haven't just been sleeping on the job, either. Her mistake was crafting that weapon with a metallic element. No metal-based object can harm my skin anymore. Not an ogre's machete nor a fine sewing needle."

"Wha…?" Eugeo grunted, still lying on the floor.

No metal weapons could hurt her? If that was true, then not only was Cardinal's dagger powerless, but so was any other kind of sword. Assuming the strange purple film that had rebuffed the tip of his dagger earlier was that protective sacred art, he couldn't begin to guess what precise art it was, in order to undo it—to say nothing of the fact that Eugeo himself did not have the skill for it.

He palmed his weapon, which was small enough to hide there, and stared up at the floating pontifex, unable to do anything else.

The naked woman whispered, "You poor thing."

"…"

"I made a promise to you. All you had to do was give your everything to me, and I would love you back. And when the eternal love you always wanted, the eternal rule, was nearly in your grasp, you chose to do *this*."

"………Eternal…love…," Eugeo repeated, hardly knowing what he was doing. "Eternal………rule……"

She nodded, playing with the Piety Module she'd just pulled from his forehead. "That's right, Eugeo. If you give your all over to me, the thirst that has tormented you your entire life will be quenched. The troubles and fears you've been grappling with all this time will go away…This is your final chance, Eugeo. Use the sword in your left hand to shatter the toy in your right. Then I shall forgive your sins with the bounty of my love."

"…"

From his prone position, Eugeo looked first at the Blue Rose Sword, then at the copper-colored dagger. Then he looked up at Administrator and said, "Love is ruling and being ruled…? The only one I feel pity for is *you*, if that is the only way you can describe it."

"…"

Now it was her turn to have no response.

All it would take was a swing of her slender hand to call down a high-level sacred art that would eliminate his life value in an instant. But Eugeo continued talking.

"I'm certain…that you must've felt the same way. Starved and searching for love…but never finding it," he continued, but on the inside, he was reflecting.

Maybe I was a child who never found love from his own parents. But even if that's true, I have loved many people in my life.

Old Man Garitta, the previous carver. Sister Azalia from the Church. Selka the apprentice sister. Grandfather, who told me stories of the past. My elder sister, Celinia, who cared for me when I was little. Vanot and Triza Walde from the farm. Their twin daughters, Teline and Telure. Golgorosso, who helped train me. Miss Azurica, the dorm manager. Tiese, who filled my life with smiles for the short time that she was my page. Ronie, who was the page of my partner.

And Kirito.

And…Alice.

"You're wrong, you wretched soul." Eugeo stared into those mysterious rainbow eyes of Administrator's, emphasizing each and every sentence. "Ruling is not loving. Love isn't transactional; you don't give it to get something in return. You give it continuously and selflessly, like water to a flower…That's what love is."

Administrator listened, a faint smile playing around her lips again. But there was no honeyed sweetness there anymore.

"…What a shame. I was going to forgive the little criminal who betrayed the Axiom Church and rescue his soul, and this is what I get in return."

And to Eugeo's breathless awe, the silver-haired young woman floating in the air changed from human to god.

There was no change to her appearance. But her unblemished white skin filled with a kind of bottomless force, a holy aura. Something in the air spoke of unfathomable power—that of a simple twitch of a finger capable of tearing the greatest warrior or arts caster to pieces.

"Eugeo…are you under the impression that I need you? That if I really want you to be my knight, I wouldn't dare take your life?"

There was no discernible emotion in her smile. All he could do was clutch his dagger even harder and bear the incredible pressure suffocating his body.

"Hee-hee…I don't need boring little boys like you. I'll suck out all your life, convert your body into a tiny jewel, and lock you away in a box. That way, even after I file away today's memories, at least I'll *feel* something when I look at it," she gloated, crossing her legs as she sat on her invisible chair.

It wasn't a bluff. If she decided she would do it, it would happen without pause.

He couldn't run away now, even if there was actually a way out. It'd take far too long for the levitating disc to take him down to the next floor. If he could somehow break the window behind him, all that awaited him outside was empty air until he hit the ground hundreds of mels below.

Besides, Eugeo's fate had been decided the moment he'd used his Perfect Weapon Control on Kirito and Alice down below. He had to stick Cardinal's dagger into the pontifex, even if the act killed him.

She was protected by a barrier that rebuffed all metal weapons. But he got the feeling that it wasn't as absolute in power as she said it was. When he had used all his strength to push in the dagger, it looked like the barrier itself had exploded. He doubted it was the end of the sacred art, but perhaps the dagger could reach her body right after a blast.

"Oh…are you still going to try something?" murmured Administrator, staring down at her prone foe. "How very thoughtful of you to keep trying to entertain me to the bitter end. Hmm, maybe it *would* be a waste to kill you and turn you into a jewel. Perhaps I could force-synthesize you, like I did her…it'll just take a while."

Despite the desperate circumstances, something in what she said stuck in Eugeo's ear. "Like…her…?"

The silver-haired woman smiled and nodded. "That's right. The one you're so infatuated with: Thirty. She really didn't want to say the words, so I had the automated senate facility undo her protection. It took several days. I was asleep, so I didn't see it for myself, but I'm sure it was torturous. What do you think? Would you like to try undergoing the same thing…?"

"…Thirty…? Alice…," he hissed.

As usual, he understood less than half of what Administrator was saying, but he could tell one thing.

Eight years ago, after she'd been tied up and taken to Central Cathedral by force, Alice had undergone a harrowing process to become an Integrity Knight. She hadn't given in to the demand to say the Remove Core Protection command the way that Eugeo had, and as a result, they'd had to pry open the door to her mind by force. Surely the wounds that Eugeo had suffered along the way were nothing in comparison to that.

No, he couldn't run away now.

He couldn't allow himself to fall without striking back at Administrator.

"……"

Eugeo clenched his teeth and pushed himself up with trembling arms, getting to his unsteady feet.

He stared back into those silvery eyes, which were losing their mirth, wrapped the chain of the dagger around his right wrist, and grabbed the hilt of the Blue Rose Sword with the same hand.

The familiar white leather clung to his palm. He drew the blade and tossed the sheath aside.

In the light of the moon from over his shoulder, the weapon shone pale and bright.

Ten mels away, the girl seated in the air narrowed her eyes in response to the light. When she spoke, her tone was noticeably more chilling.

"So that is your answer, boy. Fine…then I will at least ensure that your end is not painful."

She raised her right hand and pointed her index finger at Eugeo. Clearly, the pontifex did not need to speak the command words aloud to use sacred arts. But there were still two steps that had to be taken to use any kind of attacking art—

—the creation and processing of elements. Whether heat, ice, or some other natural force, even the greatest master needed at least two seconds to create the elements and give them a shape.

So by the time she started to move her finger, Eugeo already had the sword propped up near his shoulder.

Light-green color infused the Blue Rose Sword. Pale-blue dots appeared at the end of Administrator's finger.

"Yaaaah!"

This would be his final swing, Eugeo knew, as he launched himself off the ground. The last ultimate technique.

The Aincrad-style charging attack Sonic Leap.

In his ears, he heard Kirito's voice: *Listen, Eugeo, these techniques will move our bodies for us. But just letting it do all the work isn't going to cut it. You have to become one with the technique and speed it up with your legs and arms. If you can do that, your sword can hit the enemy before the breeze itself.*

How many times had he practiced it? How many times had he failed and wound up with his face planted firmly in the grass?

And how many times had Kirito laughed with delight…?

Eugeo's sword flashed the color of fresh green shoots and cut through the air so fast, even the sound couldn't keep up.

Administrator's smile vanished. She spread the fingers of her right hand. The ice elements, which were just about to be shot like needles, burst as they touched the Blue Rose Sword. Then Eugeo's most powerful technique smashed against Administrator's palm—or more accurately, the thin purple barrier about five cens in front of it.

He was buffeted by a shock far greater than the one earlier.

The purple barrier did succeed at blocking the accelerated Sonic Leap, but the fine layer of tiny sacred script that composed it rippled and shook.

If he kept pushing with all his might, the barrier should explode, as it had a few minutes earlier. He just had to resist it somehow and use the dagger hanging from his wrist to stab her this time. His body could disintegrate *after* that was done.

"Break...through...!!" he snarled, throwing all his strength into the still-glowing sword.

"...!"

The pontifex said nothing, but she certainly wasn't smiling anymore. Colorful light swirled deep in her narrowed eyes. Her extended fingers were all bent and strained.

She wasn't attacking with her left hand, because it was still holding the Piety Module. If she wasn't discarding that despite her insistence that she would kill him, it meant that she hadn't given up on making him a knight or that she had some other use for him.

But it was pointless to consider that now. All that mattered was completing this final attack—whether or not it required the very last drop of his strength and life.

"*Rrraaaahhh!!*"

He unleashed a bellow from the very pit of his stomach—and then, once again, something he never could have predicted happened:

The Blue Rose Sword began to sink into the purple barrier.

The wall itself was not gone. But the tip of the sword was indeed cutting—no, slipping through—the layer of sacred script that was supposed to rebuff all metal.

It wasn't a trick of the eyes. Even the mirrors on Administrator's face were gaping.

The situation abruptly changed.

Administrator stopped attempting to hold back Eugeo's sword and suddenly leaped back. The barrier retreated with her, and without the surface holding it in place, the Blue Rose Sword swung downward with a slicing whoosh. The moment the edge touched the ground, a gash several mels long opened in the thick carpet.

He couldn't tell what had happened. All he knew was that if he stayed where he was, her attack art would hit him. His limbs felt heavy after summoning all that power, but he promptly bolted into action regardless.

This time, his enemy was faster. As she pulled back, the pontifex generated fresh elements and sent them hurtling at Eugeo. By the time he was in his technique stance, green lights were flying right at him.

On instinct, Eugeo broke the stance and used the Blue Rose Sword to block his body. The wind elements burst with a flash, and the ensuing gust of wind pushed Eugeo against the south wall again.

Fortunately for him, she had forgone the step of shaping the elements. If she'd turned them into blades of wind rather than just dispersing the energy in the motes of light themselves, he could've easily lost a limb.

But not all his luck was good. Rather than slamming into the flat glass windowpane, this time Eugeo's back struck one of the large pillars that connected the windows. It was designed with a massive standing sword motif, and Eugeo smashed into the side of the blade before falling to the ground. If that had been the naked edge, it might have maimed him, even though the sword was only decorative. Maybe that made him lucky after all, but the pain was enough to drive the breath from his lungs.

I have to move. It'll be real sacred arts next time, he told himself, lifting his upper half off the ground.

She had retreated to the other side of the bed; the only thing he could see in the darkness was the shine of her silver hair. She was far away enough to be out of range of his Sonic Leap—but it was an easy distance for a sacred art. If he didn't get off the ground, he would die.

"Nnh...hrrg..."

Somehow, he got to one knee. But there was no strength to push off with. He tried and tried to stand, but the leg only trembled and refused to obey.

No. Not yet. I can't give up now. Why did I even come back to this room, then?

What have I been living for all this time?

"Grr...raaaahh!"

Eugeo pressed his back against the golden sword decoration and used his Blue Rose Sword as a support to get to his feet. He could tell that the previous impact had cut him as well as buffeted him, because there were droplets of blood spattering on the floor below.

It must've taken well over five seconds for him to get up, but for some reason, Administrator wasn't attacking. She just floated in the darkness twenty mels away, holding her silence.

In time, he heard an utterance so quiet that it would have been inaudible if not in the midst of absolute silence.

"......That sword...Ah, now I see..."

Eugeo glanced down at his blades, uncertain of what she meant. The Blue Rose Sword was thrust tip down into the floor. Hanging from his wrist was the little copper dagger. Which of the two was she referring to?

His intuition told him this was a crucial distinction, but before he could reach an answer, the quiet that filled the top floor of Central Cathedral was broken by neither Eugeo nor Administrator.

"Ah, ah, aiiiieeeee!!"

It was coming from a circle in the floor about five mels away that was now sinking out of sight—the platform to the floor below. The voice was louder now that there was just a dark portal in the middle of the carpet.

"H-h-help meeeee, Your Holiness!!" wailed the voice, which clearly belonged to Prime Senator Chudelkin, who had gone down to the ninety-ninth floor earlier. Administrator proceeded forward through the darkness in silence and stood at the edge of the bed.

"...What is it about him that grows more childish with age? Perhaps it's nearly time to reset him," she muttered, shaking her head. Eyeing her with caution, Eugeo stealthily backed away toward the west wall, putting distance between himself and the hole.

The disc was sinking but not very fast. It would take most of a minute for it to descend all the way to the floor, then rise again with Chudelkin atop it.

But no sooner was there a twenty-cen space between the floor and the disc than two pale, clammy hands grasped the edges of the aperture.

"Hohhhhh!!" he screeched, and his round head appeared. The perfectly hairless skin was bright red now. The prime senator squeezed and pulled until his body popped through and landed on the floor.

His clothes hadn't changed since he'd left the room earlier, gloating. But now, the puffed-out red-and-blue clown outfit was torn and sliced all over and slightly deflated. He plopped down on the carpet, wheezing and puffing.

Administrator gazed at him coldly. "What happened to your clothes?"

Meanwhile, Eugeo was stunned. The arms and torso that were visible through the ends of the prime senator's tattered clothing were as thin as gnarled branches. And yet his head was as puffed up and round as ever—like a child's drawing of a stick figure with a circle head.

So what did it mean that the first time he'd seen the man in the great bath, the clown's outfit was puffed up to bursting? As Eugeo wondered, Chudelkin got to his feet, seeming not to notice the presence of the young man, and tried desperately to plead his case.

"Y-Your Holiness, I am certain that my appearance must be most displeasing to you, but I assure you, it is the result of a ferocious battle in which I endeavored to punish the rebels and protect the glory of the great Axiom Church!"

At that point, Chudelkin must have realized the pontifex was completely nude, because his crescent-shaped eyes went full moon. He slapped his hands over his face, giant head turning even redder.

"Hohhh! Oh-hoooo!! Oh, you mustn't! Your Holiness, I am entirely unworthy of your visage! My eyeballs shall explode! I shall turn into stoooone!!" he wailed, but despite his protestations, the gaps between his fingers were wide, and his beady eyes gleamed through them.

Administrator covered her cheek with her hand and threatened, "If you don't state your business, I really will turn you to stone."

"Hohhh! Hwaaaa...ah...aaah!" screeched Chudelkin, immediately stopping his contortions and freezing in place. His burning-red head promptly went pale. The prime senator suddenly spun on his heel and hopped like a frog toward the hole he'd just climbed through. The platform was still down on the ninety-ninth floor and hadn't returned yet.

"W-we must seal this place at once! They're coming! The devils!!"

"...You mean you didn't eliminate the rebels?" Administrator asked.

Chudelkin's back twitched. "W-w-w-well, I fought valiantly and with great sacrifice, as you can see from my condition, but these rebellious devils are most foul and treacherous and sadistic...," he screeched.

In the back of his mind, Eugeo considered this information.

The "rebels" Chudelkin spoke of were obviously Kirito and Alice, whom he'd left trapped in ice down there. No matter that the prime senator was the second-greatest user of sacred arts in the Church or that the others were trapped in ice—Eugeo couldn't imagine them being defeated. Sure enough, they'd put up a fierce fight that apparently had sent him running wounded.

However, that meant…

Eugeo subconsciously retreated a few steps from the platform hole. He must've caused some slight rustling of fabric, because Chudelkin paused in the midst of his excuses and glanced his way.

Those thin, beady eyes were wide again. The prime senator thrust his finger at Eugeo, instantly forgetting his own miserable failure, and screamed, "Hwaaaa! Y-you! Number Thirty-Two! What in the world are you doing there?! H-h-how dare you draw your sword in the Chamber of the Gods, where Her Holiness dwells! You will crawl upon the ground, *this instant!*"

"………"

But Eugeo barely heard anything Chudelkin said anymore. His ears were fixed on a faint vibrating sound coming up from the floor below. The sound of the thick levitating disc rising through the power of sacred arts.

Belatedly, the prime senator noticed it, too, in between his seething insults, and he fell silent. Then he turned around, got down on all fours, and peered into the hole in the carpet.

"Hwaaaaaa!!" he screamed, his loudest yet, and turned back to Eugeo. "N-N-N-Number Thirty-Two! What are you doing?! Go! Go now! This only happened because *you* failed to rough them up enough! This isn't my job! Y-Your Holiness, surely you must know th……."

Chudelkin was crawling toward the bed, babbling furiously the entire time, until a hand reached up through the hole in the floor and grabbed his right foot.

"Eeeeeeek!!" he squealed, eyes bulging, and kicked his legs. The pointed clown shoe popped off, and the momentum caused his little body to roll. The prime senator leaped to his feet, bounded for the bed, peeled the hanging canopy curtain aside, and wriggled into the darkness between it and the floor.

The pontifex, who was standing on the bed, stared down at the hole in the floor with a smile on her face, all thought of the prime senator's miserable state banished. Eugeo was prepared to attack at once if she showed hostility, but for now she seemed content to wait for her guest to appear.

Eugeo glanced back at the levitating platform. The hand that had grasped Chudelkin's shoe was still fully extended. The black sleeve slid downward, revealing an arm that was thin but finely muscled.

How many times had those arms saved Eugeo?

In fact, for as long as he could remember, he'd been led around by that hand. Even now, after Eugeo had gone the wrong way and turned his sword on the owner of that arm, the advance continued.

The disc continued rising.

Next to appear was black hair, still tousled from battle. Then two eyes darker than the night sky beyond the windows and yet brighter than the stars. Lastly, a mouth curved into a cocky grin...

".........Kirito..."

Eugeo's voice was trembling. It wasn't loud enough to be audible over ten mels away, but his friend glanced toward him along the wall anyway and nodded, smile never wavering.

It was a gesture that was warm and heartening, just like all the ones he'd made since the moment they'd met. The disc finally came to a heavy, grinding stop.

Kirito...there you are...

Something deep inside him throbbed with an emotion he couldn't even name.

But that pain wasn't an unpleasant one. It was certainly much gentler than the suffering he'd felt when the Piety Module was jammed into his head—and more wistful and sweet.

As he watched, frozen in place, his partner and teacher dressed in black smirked and said, "Yo, Eugeo."

"……I told you not to come," he murmured.

His partner hurled Chudelkin's silly shoe and beamed even harder.

"When have I ever followed the instructions you gave to me?"

"……Good point. You've always………been like……"

He couldn't find the words.

He meant to pay for the crime of attacking his friend by sacrificing his life. He was going to use that secret weapon from Cardinal to pierce Administrator's skin, even if he had to get torn to pieces to do it. And now he was reunited with Kirito again, without having completed this duty.

But no. It was Kirito's own will that had brought him here.

He'd broken through Eugeo's Perfect Control art, defeated Prime Senator Chudelkin, and reached the hundredth floor while Eugeo was still alive.

Yes, I'm still alive. And I still have the dagger hanging from my wrist. Which means now is the time to fight. That's the one thing I can do.

Eugeo turned away from his partner and looked to the center of the chamber. Administrator waited on the massive bed, an enigmatic smile playing across her lips. Her mirror eyes caught the moonlight but, as usual, did not reveal any emotion of their own. All that was clear was that she was watching this new visitor and thinking about something.

He had to explain to Kirito before the battle resumed. He had to tell him that her flesh was protected by a barrier that blocked all metal—and that it wasn't infallible.

Without taking his eyes off the pontifex, Eugeo began moving toward his partner.

Just then, there was the sound of metal shifting from the direction he was moving. He had to break his gaze to look over.

To Kirito's right, another figure strode forward from the thick shadow cast by the pillar between the windowpanes.

Golden hair and armor sparkled in the light of the moon. At the left side of the figure's waist was the Osmanthus Blade, a Divine Object with a hilt fashioned like flower petals. A white skirt billowed below.

The Integrity Knight Alice Synthesis Thirty.

Eugeo had seen her working with Kirito already on the ninety-ninth floor. But seeing them standing together like this made his chest throb even harder. His legs stopped moving toward Kirito of their own accord.

Alice stared at the pontifex, then at Eugeo.

The right side of her face was covered in the dark bandage still. Integrity Knights were known for being excellent arts casters, so she should have been able to heal her eye in an instant. Perhaps she was leaving it as it was in *order* to feel the pain.

Her deep-blue left eye was full of conflicting emotions as she looked over Eugeo. It wasn't at all like the impassive, cold gaze she'd had down on the eightieth floor. This time, it was full of human emotion.

She hadn't recovered her Alice Zuberg memories yet, but there had been massive change within Alice the knight in a short amount of time. And the obvious cause of that was the black-haired swordsman standing next to her. Kirito's words had pierced the unmeltable ice that surrounded her heart.

And if, somehow, they could recover the memory fragment that Administrator was hiding somewhere in this room and return Alice to her old self, then Alice the knight would go back to being Alice Zuberg, Eugeo's childhood friend.

And it meant that Alice the knight, the one who had spoken to Kirito, sheathed her sword, and withstood the pain of losing her eye in order to fight back against the Axiom Church, would vanish.

That was Eugeo's greatest wish and the reason he had fought so hard to get here. But how did the present Alice understand this? And Kirito…He had fought to the death against Vice Commander Fanatio, only to save her life afterward. Did he really desire for Alice the knight to be eliminated forever...?

Eugeo took a deep breath, let it out, and forced himself to stop thinking about it. He had to focus on this, the final fight. He'd been able to let his mind wander because Administrator was passively letting the situation play out, but she could resume attacking at any time.

He tore his eyes from Alice and looked back at the center of the room, resuming his march. He sidled across the moonlit floor until he was next to Kirito at last. Then he pressed the Blue Rose Sword into the floor again with a sharp exhale, resting his weight on it.

"Are you hurt?" Kirito whispered. "It's not...my fault, is it?"

"..."

The fact that his partner was willing to let that simple statement cover *everything* that had happened on the floor below them brought an unexpected smile to Eugeo's lips.

"You never hit me with your sword, not once. I had a run-in with a pillar."

"You could've waited until we got up here."

"...I was the one who trapped you to keep you down there, Kirito."

"As if I was weak enough that something like that would stop me." Kirito snorted.

Bantering with him like this reminded Eugeo of before they'd split apart at the eightieth floor...like the times back at the dorm of the academy. The throbbing in his chest lessened just a bit.

But what happened had happened and would never go away. He had given in to Administrator's temptations and attacked his best friend, a crime that no amount of words would lessen.

Eugeo pursed his lips and gripped the hilt of his sword. Kirito stared at the middle of the room until eventually he muttered, "Is that Administrator? The pontifex of the Church?"

"That's right," came the answer from Kirito's other side. "She hasn't changed at all in the last six years," Alice stated.

After this direct mention, Administrator finally broke her long silence.

"Oh, my…I've never had so many guests in this chamber at one time. Do I recall, Chudelkin, that you insisted I leave the fate of Alice and the irregular boy to you?"

The curtains hanging around the side of the bed parted from the inside, and a very large head popped out. Prime Senator Chudelkin rubbed his forehead nervously and craned his neck at an angle that suggested he'd made some kind of mistake.

"Hoh, hoh-hee! W-w-w-well, I assure you, Your Holiness, I fought as bravely as a lion for your sake…"

"You mentioned that already."

"Hwaaaa! I-it is not my fault, oh-hooo! Number Thirty-Two was sloppy and only half encased them in the ice…And Number Thirty, that hideous gold knight, had the gall to utilize her Memory Release ability on me! Though I'm not so flimsy as to let that gaudy little princess's secret technique put a single scratch on me, hoh-hee-hee-hee!"

"Anyone but him," Alice muttered darkly.

Chudelkin didn't notice—he spun around and looked up at Administrator, who was standing upon the bed, and screeched, "In fact, it was Number One and Number Two who started it by going mad! I can only assume that their idiocy has now infected Number Thirty!"

"Ah…now be quiet," Administrator commanded. Chudelkin shut his mouth and froze where he lay on the floor. But he kept his eyes wide open, which he seemed to be doing in order to drink in the sight of the pontifex's nakedness.

Administrator's silver eyes were fixed on Alice and totally unconcerned with whatever the prime senator was doing. She inclined her head in curiosity.

"It was about time for me to reset Bercouli and Fanatio anyway…but I've only had you for six years, yes, Alice? You don't seem to have any errors in your logic circuits…So is it the influence of that irregular unit next to you? Fascinating."

Eugeo didn't understand anything of what she was saying. But there was something in the silver-haired woman's tone of voice that made him shiver—like a shepherd speaking about a sheep or a craftswoman about her tools.

"Well, Alice? Do you have something you want to say to me? I won't be angry. Go ahead and speak your mind," Administrator said with a faint smile, taking a step forward atop the bed.

Alice took a similar step backward, as though pushed by an invisible wall. To his surprise, Eugeo saw that the knight's profile looked even paler than the moonlight, and her lips were clenched shut. But Alice stood firm and reached up with her bare hand to touch the bandage over her right eye. Then her withdrawn leg took a step forward instead, as if the scrap of cloth had given her strength.

Tak.

The sound of her foot was sharp and crisp, as though there wasn't any carpet underneath. The golden knight, instead of kneeling before her master, thrust her chest forward and declared, "Holy Pontifex, the proud order of Integrity Knights has been shattered. It was defeated at the hand of the two rebels beside me...as well as the boundless obsession and deceit that *you* have built with this tower!!"

CHAPTER THIRTEEN

FINAL BATTLE, MAY 380 HE

1

Ooh, well said.

Given the weight of the situation, I suppose my own reaction was a bit less than totally serious. But if I didn't treat it that lightly, the freezing tone would have overwhelmed me and caused me to back down.

When we arrived at the hundredth floor of Central Cathedral at last, it was a circular chamber well over a hundred feet across. In the middle of the room was a massive circular bed, and that seemed to be the only piece of furniture.

And atop the bed, without a stitch of clothing covering her body, was a breathtakingly beautiful woman.

She was, without a doubt, the absolute ruler of the Axiom Church and thus of the human race as a whole: Administrator. But her sense of presence was so great that just by standing there, she made me instantly lose sight of the fact that this was actually a virtual world called the Underworld and that she and all the other people here were "artificial fluctlights," AI routines saved on an artificial medium in the real world.

But in fact, I didn't need to see her brilliant silvery hair and mirrorlike eyes first. From the moment I'd first stepped onto the platform that would take me up to this floor, my palms had been sweaty, and cold fear had gripped my spine. As I had looked through the hole in the ceiling directly above me and into the darkness that awaited, I had felt an aura of death more thick and cold than in any of the boss chambers in the original Aincrad.

The real me—not Kirito the elite disciple but the actual Kazuto Kirigaya—wouldn't die inside The Soul Translator if I lost all my life value here in the Underworld. But the entity known as Administrator had the ability to inflict suffering on me that far surpassed death.

In fact, hadn't Cardinal said that Administrator wasn't bound by the Taboo Index she herself had created but instead was still restricted by the conceptual taboos that she'd been raised with? That murder was the one thing she couldn't commit?

But because of that limitation, she could inflict pain that was far more horrible than logging out of the Underworld—I could wind up like those senators, living like a machine hooked up to a feeding tube, forever.

Of course, just because I understood more about the underlying situation than Alice or Eugeo did didn't mean that my fear was greater than theirs.

Administrator had removed Eugeo's Piety Module herself, but Alice's was still embedded in her fluctlight. I couldn't begin to imagine how frightening it must have been for her to face off against her absolute ruler.

And yet the golden knight held her head high and proud as she declared, "My ultimate duty is not the protection of the Axiom Church! It is to protect the peaceful labor and rest of the unarmed multitudes! And your actions, more than any other thing, threaten the peace and safety of the people of the world!!"

Alice's golden hair shone, lit with righteous purpose. Her voice cut crisply through the heavy, cold gloom, keeping it at bay.

But the pontifex didn't express any anger at Alice's bold castigation. If anything, her lips curled with entertainment. Instead, it was Prime Senator Chudelkin—who was hiding under the bed for some reason—whose hideous screeching voice rent the air.

"S-s-sileeeeence!!"

He hurtled out of the hanging sheet and performed a series of somersaults before popping to his feet. He wobbled a bit from all the rotation but recovered to express his full indignation in the space between us and the pontifex.

His red-and-blue outfit was torn to shreds, and the poison gas he'd used on the previous floor was gone, thanks to Alice's Perfect Weapon Control of the Osmanthus Blade. That skill had split the blade into hundreds of tiny pieces that whirled into an astonishing storm of petals that were meant to help us escape Eugeo's ice—Chudelkin got caught in the aftermath only because he came chortling down from the ceiling at the right time.

As usual, his slipperiness was impressive. Despite the damage to his clothes, he retreated without suffering much injury himself, but now, on the top floor, there was no escape. With the mighty Administrator behind him, however, he was bold again, throwing his hands into the air and then jutting both pointer fingers at Alice.

"Why, you half-broken little toy knight! Your *duty*?! To *protect*?! How you make me laugh! Hohhhh-hoh-hoh-hoh-hohhhhh!!"

He did a little spin, causing the tattered shreds of his clothing to lift up into the air, exposing striped red-and-blue underpants. Then he put his hands on his hips and stuck out his left foot at her this time. "You knights are nothing more than puppets that act on my command!! If I tell you to lick my boot, you will lick it! If I say that you are my steed, you will carry me on your back!! *That* is the duty you knights are blessed to have!!"

He lost his balance and nearly toppled over backward due to his massive head, but the wild swinging of his arms helped him stay on his feet.

"More importantly," he continued, "the idea that the knighthood is destroyed is absolute poppycock! Less than ten overall, including the worthless old Number One and Two, were damaged at all! In other words, I have more than twenty pawns still remaining! One single member mouthing off does not even *begin* to affect the ironclad rule of the Church, you hideous, shining wench!!"

Ironically, the clown's vulgar insults succeeded only at calming Alice's nerves. She was back to her sharp, rational nature. With a shake of her head, she said, "You are the fool here, scarecrow. Are there brains in that oversize head of yours, or just straw and scraps of cloth?"

"Wha…whaaaaa—?!"

The blood rushed to his crimson head until he was fully purple. But before he could scream whatever came to his mind, Alice icily continued, "Of the remaining twenty knights, half of them are immobile at the moment, due to the pontifex's so-called reset to modify their memories with sacred arts. And the other half are on their dragons, fighting at the End Mountains. You cannot call them back here now. If you did, the forces of darkness would immediately pile through the caves in the north, west, and south parts of the mountains, as well as the Eastern Gate, and cause the Axiom Church's rule to crumble."

"Nng…hrrgg…!"

Chudelkin's face was now turning from purple to black. But Alice wasn't done yet.

"In fact, it is already crumbling. Those ten knights and their dragons cannot fight forever. But the cathedral no longer has any knights in reserve to replace them. Or will you venture into the Dark Territory yourself, Chudelkin, and bravely battle with the fearsome dark knights?"

I couldn't help but feel a bit self-conscious about that remark. The backup knights—like Eldrie and Deusolbert and the Four Whirling Blades—had just been hospitalized because of Eugeo and me.

Still, out of the corner of my eye, I caught sight of Chudelkin's head reaching the limit of its internal pressure.

"Mwa-hohhhhh!! You—you—you sneaky little—!! Do you think you've gotten the better of us with that, you miserable whelp?!" he screamed, like a kettle letting off steam, his feet stomping the floor in a childish tantrum. "As punishment for this absolute insolence, you'll be sent to the mountains for three years once you've been reset! Oh, but before all of that, I'll keep you for my personal plaything!!"

He began to screech about exactly the sorts of things that he would force Alice to do, until a word from Administrator behind him instantly shut him up.

"...Hmm."

He went stock-still and silent, his face returning to its original color. The pontifex ignored him and turned to Alice. "No, it doesn't seem to be a logic-circuit error. And your Piety Module is still functional...Does that mean you independently removed the Code 871 that was installed for me...? And not just on a sudden emotional burst...?"

What is she talking about? I wondered, scowling. *Installed? By whom...? Code Eight-Seven-One...?*

The silver-haired young woman was not forthcoming with more information, however. She swept the hair hanging on her shoulders back and changed gears. "Well, I won't know any more than that without a good analysis. Now, Chudelkin...I am a generous person, so I will give you an opportunity to improve your now miserable reputation. Use your abilities to freeze those three. You can reduce their life to, oh, let's say twenty percent."

When she was done speaking, she waved her right pointer finger. Instantly, the massive bed beneath her feet rumbled into rotation. My eyes bugged out.

Like an enormous screw, the forty-foot-wide bed began to descend into the floor. Chudelkin squealed and darted away from it.

Eventually, the entire bed had fit itself snugly into the floor, even the hanging canopy, such that there was nothing but carpet with a large circle drawn on it. A moment later, Administrator descended to the floor without a sound.

On a sudden whim, I glanced down at my own feet and saw that there was a similar circle in the carpet where the levitating disc had brought us up. I guessed that the room must be designed so that everything extended and retracted into the floor that way, but a glance around the room revealed that there was only one other circle, a small one on the far wall across from us. I couldn't begin to guess what it contained.

Once the bed was gone, the top floor of the tower seemed shockingly vast.

The circular walls were all made of perfectly unblemished, crystal clear glass, meaning that only the golden pillars supported the domed ceiling. The dome was decorated with art that seemed to be depicting the genesis of the world, and crystals affixed all over the display blinked and glimmered like stars.

What did surprise me was the sword-themed golden decorations that adorned all the pillars. The smaller ones were still over three feet long, and the longest nearly ten. The hilts were quite small, though, so it was clearly impossible to pull them off the wall and use them as weapons. The edges didn't look very sharp, either.

Otherwise, the hundredth floor of the cathedral was the worst kind of place to fight someone who could cast sacred arts: wide open with nothing to hide behind. I put weight into my right foot, preparing to leap forward on Chudelkin before he could start chanting.

But before I could execute my plan, Alice shook her head. "It's dangerous to just charge in. The pontifex will have an art that can capture us alive if she simply touches us. The reason she allowed Chudelkin to go first is undoubtedly to give herself a better chance to make contact with us."

"Now that you mention it," Eugeo whispered, the first thing he'd said in ages, "I have a feeling that she chose not to kill me, when she certainly could have. And when the prime senator turned Bercouli to stone, he was riding on him...touching him directly."

"Okay," I said, nodding. "So it works on contact with the target."

Propelled attack arts like fireballs or ice blades notwithstanding, any kind of art that had a specific target, as a general rule, required that the caster make contact with that target, even if just on the leg or foot. It was one of the fundamental rules of the sacred arts that any novice at the academy would learn.

In other words, as long as we didn't let Chudelkin or Administrator actually touch us, we didn't have to worry about falling prey to that horrifying petrification ability. But at the same time, that meant we couldn't get within sword-swinging range.

That ultimately left us at a disadvantage. In terms of sacred arts, Eugeo and I were nothing compared to Alice, and in a battle of long-distance attacks, even the three of us together were likely to get outgunned against the prime senator.

I bit my lip, thinking hard. Eugeo continued, "Plus...the pontifex has a full-body—"

Whatever he was trying to say got cut off by Chudelkin, who sprang up from his sitting position. "Hoh-hoh-hohhh!"

We took fighting stances in reaction. He gave us a suddenly very nasty smile, then turned back to his commander and simpered, "You can flatten those three little dung beetles with the press of your pinky finger, Your Holiness, yet you bestowed upon me the honor and pleasure of dealing with them! I might cry! I do believe I shall!! Hoo-goo, hoo-goo-goo-goo..."

Sure enough, sticky tears began gushing from the corners of his eyes, forming large droplets that tumbled off his cheeks. It was sickening.

Even Administrator seemed tired of dealing with him. She backed away about twenty feet and said impatiently, "Fine. Just do it."

"Yeh-heh-hes, Your Holiness! I shall undertake every last effort to meet your satisfactiooooon!"

He pushed both thumbs into his temples as if there were buttons there, and his tears instantly stopped. The little clown leered at us and continued, "Now, now, now...You will not get off with simple apologies. No, I'll be grinding down nearly all of your life before I finally allow you to sob and beg on your knees. Are you ready for that? Are you *sure*?"

"...I'm tired of listening to your nonsense. Just do your worst already. Like I said on the floor below, I'm ready to cut that filthy tongue clean out of your hideous mouth," snapped Alice, who was not one to lose the war of words. She squeezed the hilt of her sword and widened her stance.

About fifty feet away, Chudelkin took an odd stance of his own, crossing his arms in front of his chest.

"Ohhhhhh, you'll get it now!! If you want my beautiful, perfect tongue, you'll have it—sliding all over your body, once I've frozen you in solid ice!! *Hwaaaaa!!*" he screamed, and launched himself into a magnificent leap, performing a one-and-a-half backflip with a full twist and landing hard. Not on his feet or his hands but on the top of his head.

"......"

Neither I, Eugeo, nor Alice said a word. Yes, it made sense that with his enormous head and spindly body, the prime senator would find it more stable to be situated upside down, but what was he going to do now that he was stuck there?

But Chudelkin maintain a firmly serious expression—as far as I could tell, since it was hard to read it upside down—extended his arms and legs, and screeched, "System...Caaaaall!!"

Alice promptly drew her blade. Eugeo and I took stances as well, though we weren't sure what to do yet.

"Generrrate Crrryogenic Element!!" he cried, enthusiastically rolling his *r*'s.

The power and scale of a long-range attack art could be narrowed down to a fairly specific window based on the number of elements that were initially generated. I watched closely, determined to spot exactly how many little ice lights appeared in his fingers.

Paaam!! Chudelkin clapped his hands together and spread them wide, still upside down. At the ends of his fingers, thrumming softly, were ten little motes of blue light.

"Damn, the maximum," I cursed, but it wasn't unexpected. I was barely more than a beginner, and even I could generate five elements at a time on one hand if I focused hard enough. Chudelkin was the greatest caster in the Axiom Church after Administrator, so making five on each hand would be second nature to him.

Alice didn't move, but I took a step to the right and held up my off hand in order to generate the opposing heat elements. Eugeo took the exact same stance. If we each made five, perhaps we could defend ourselves against Chudelkin's ice…

But right as I was about to give the command, there was another dry *paaam!!*

It was Chudelkin, this time smacking his bare feet together. Then he spread his legs wide until they were straight lines along with his arms. With the sound of dewdrops falling, ten little ice elements appeared over the tips of his toes.

Eugeo's hoarse whisper spoke for the both of us.

"…You gotta be…kidding me…"

With twenty elements in total now floating off his hands and feet, Chudelkin's upside-down mouth curved into a huge grin.

"Oh-ho, oh-ho-ho-ho-ho…Very frightened, are we? Peeing our pants just a little, hmm? If you assumed I was no different from any of those measly arts casters, you were very wrong."

The Underworld's concept of sacred arts—in short, magic—was confined by vocal commands and the imagination of the caster. For example, in the act of performing healing arts, any hostility toward the target in the heart of the caster would dramatically lessen the effectiveness of the healing. But if one prayed with all one's being for recovery, the results might actually surpass the privilege level of the caster.

Elemental attack arts worked the same way. Vocal commands— the sacred words—were not enough to alter the shape of the generated elements. They had to be linked to the image in the caster's mind for guidance.

That image was a finger. From the start to the very end of the process, the caster had to focus on the mental image of each element, connected to each finger. For this reason, even the most advanced of users could only control ten elements with ten fingers. In order to break that limit and utilize the toes for this mental image as well, you'd either have to be floating in the air off your feet somehow—or balanced on your head such that all the limbs were free. Just like Prime Senator Chudelkin.

"Oh-ho-ho-ho-ho!" he screamed, and started chanting the element-activation command at ultrahigh speed as we stood dumbfounded. First he thrust his right hand toward us, then his left.

"Dischaaaaaargeuh!!"

Shoom! Five icicles shot forth, rending the air in a vortex of chill. Cold on their heels came another five.

There was no escape. Two fanning spreads of ice spears, high and low, covered every angle. The only way out was to knock down the spears that would hit us, so I squeezed my sword hilt and focused—

Golden glimmering covered my sight.

Alice had swiped the Osmanthus Blade sideways, disintegrating the tip into a multitude of little shards that spun and danced through the air. It wasn't the first time we'd seen Alice's Perfect Weapon Control, but it still succeeded in taking our breath away with its beauty.

The only light illuminating the top floor of Central Cathedral was the moonlight coming through the windows on the southern side. But the golden petals reflected it as though they were glowing with their own light as they swarmed, creating a thick, dense meteor shower.

"Haaah!" Alice cried, swinging the hilt, which was all that was left in her hand.

The storm of petals swooped in coordination with her action, enveloping the ten icicle spears and filling the air with a tremendous grinding sound. It was as though she'd tossed ice cubes into a high-powered mixer on liquefy; in moments, Chudelkin's spears had been reduced to sherbet, melting harmlessly into the air and expending their magical resources.

"Hnng…grrrrrrng!!" the little man grunted, grinding his teeth as he witnessed his confident attack being completely nullified. "Don't think you're so special just because of your stupid little grater!" he howled. "How do you plan to handle *this*?! Hohhhhh!!"

He swung his feet, still holding ten elements of their own, from the sides to a raised position. The ice elements rose in parallel toward the ceiling, where they met and formed a square crystal block.

The ice grew and grew with a series of heavy booms, until it formed a solid cube about seven feet to a side. But its transformation didn't stop there; vicious spikes grew on every surface.

If the physical rules of the Underworld were the same as real life, the cube of ice up above had to weigh a good seven tons. Judging on the spot that it would be impossible to stop that with swords alone, I fell back a step.

"Hoh-hee-hee…How do you like that? Just one step before my ultimate sacred art!! Get ready to be *flattennned*!!"

From his headstand position, Chudelkin lowered his upright legs to a forward position. The spiked die made of ice came hurtling downward with a deafening rush.

Eugeo and I jumped sideways, desperate to get out of the way. But once again, Alice did not show an ounce of hesitation. She stared down the massive object that was about to crush her to a pulp, not moving a muscle…

"Haaaaaaaaah!!"

With the loudest and fiercest cry she'd made in any fight so far, Alice thrust the hilt of her sword high.

The storm of golden shards floating around her collected into a sharp formation with a crisp *cha-king!* They formed a huge cone about ten feet tall with the pieces arranged outward into fierce spikes. The formation spun as the block of ice descended upon it.

When the two objects collided, the vast chamber was filled with a show of sound and light that was both deafening and blinding, all at once.

"Krrrnngggg…Crush…them…flaaaaaat!"

"…Break it apart…flowers!!"

The prime senator and the Integrity Knight screamed, polar opposites of beauty and ugliness, both twisted with ferocious effort. With major works of magic like this, in addition to numerical priority, it was willpower and mental-image strength that would determine the ultimate winner.

For several seconds, the blue chunk of ice and the golden spiral held firm at equal distance from their white-hot intersection point, but they gradually grew closer. Thanks to the overwhelming light and ear-splitting roaring, it was impossible to tell whether it was the cube crushing the drill with its overwhelming weight, or the drill gouging out the ice.

Only when the two objects were nearly overlapping did it become clear which of the two had won.

With a sharp crack, the entire cube of ice split, going white. Then the block, which was the size of a small shed, burst tremendously into a vast number of little shards. The air was instantly colored white, and I had to hold up my left arm to shield myself from the onslaught of cold.

"Hkyaaaa?!" shrieked Chudelkin. His outstretched limbs trembled. "Th…this is preposterous…My superbly impressive and ultimate sacred art, which was bequeathed to me by Her Holiness…"

That mocking smile had vanished from his venomously red lips, but despite the feat of obliterating the massive ice block, Alice wasn't unscathed, either. She swung her arm to return the cone of shards to the form of her sword once again but had to valiantly hold firm to maintain her balance. I guessed that she'd probably taken some of the impact of the flying ice at close range.

"Alice!" I cried, but she held out her free hand to stop me and pointed the tip of her blade toward the distant Chudelkin.

"Chudelkin, your faithless acts are nothing more than a paper balloon filled with air—just like you!!"

"Wha…wha—*haah*—wha…?!"

Her cutting remark was so devastating that for once, the man couldn't come up with a response. His round face was distorted beyond belief and twitching violently as greasy sweat poured in rivers down his upside-down features.

Just then, Administrator broke her silence from the back of the room, speaking to her level of boredom.

"No matter how many years pass, you'll never not be stupid, Chudelkin."

The prime senator's limbs promptly withdrew. He shrank like a sulking child, while the pontifex gracefully turned on her side and lay down in the middle of the air, as though there were an invisible sofa there. She floated upward, crossed her legs, and continued, "Alice's Osmanthus Blade has the highest level of physical priority of any existing Divine Object. And she utterly believes in that fact. And yet you attempt to use a physical-type attack art against her. Have you forgotten the most basic fundamentals of sacred arts?"

"Hah…hoh-hoh-hah-hee…," Chudelkin giggled nervously. Tears burst from his eyes without warning. Since he was balancing on his head, they ran down his forehead and sank into the carpet where his scalp met it.

"Oh-hoooo…Oh, what an honor, what glory, what privilege!! Her Holiness herself, offering lessons to the lowly likes of me! I shall rise to the occasion…Humble Chudelkin will prove himself worthy of this tender mercyyyyy!!"

Somehow, Administrator's statement had been more effective than any healing art. His disbelief had been wiped clean in an instant, and the prime senator was now glaring boldly at Alice with his own bizarre brand of proud confidence.

"Number Thirty! You just likened me to a paper balloon filled with nothing but hot air!"

"…Are you saying you're not?"

"Nooooot! Not, not, not, not!!" Chudelkin's eyes seemed to light with visible flames. "I do have strong beliefs of my own!

And one of those is love!! I am driven by pure and selfless love for my wise and beauteous Holiness!!"

At any other time, in any other place, this would come off like third-rate theater. But somehow, in this moment, the statement reverberated powerfully through the room. It was almost kind of touching, in a pathetic way—even if it was coming from a half-naked clown man balancing on his oversize head.

Chudelkin glared at Alice with burning eyes, spread his limbs wide, and screeched, "Y-Y-Y-Your Holiness!!"

"What is it, Chudelkin?"

"After so many long years of faithful service, I, Prime Senator Chudelkin, do finally, for the first time, make a most impudent request of you!! I shall henceforth risk life and limb to vanquish the brazen traitors, and all that I ask—nothing more!—is that upon my successful completion of this weighty duty, I at last be allowed...to place my hands...to place my lips...upon your blessed figure...and to spend a...a...a night of dreams fulfilled together!!"

Well, that's one way to make a bold request of the absolute ruler of all humanity.

But there was clearly no doubt that this was a scream from the heart, an absolutely true confession of real emotion from the very depth of Chudelkin's soul.

It was so far beyond pathos now that it was genuinely heroic. Neither I, nor Eugeo, nor Alice could move a muscle.

Floating on the other end of the room, Administrator reacted to Chudelkin's request by...curving her pale lips into a smile that suggested nothing could be funnier. Her mirror eyes, which reflected all light, now wavered between scorn and mockery. But when she spoke, covering her mouth with her hand, the voice that emerged was full of benevolence that was at odds with her expression.

"...Very well, Chudelkin," she murmured. "I swear to Stacia, goddess of creation. When you have fulfilled your duty, you shall have an entire night to do with my body whatever you wish."

Because I came from the real world, with all its lies and deceptions, it was laughably obvious to me that she didn't mean a word of that promise.

But the people of this world, probably due to the structure of their artificial fluctlights, were unable to disobey the laws and rules that existed on a higher level of importance than them. These laws ran from local precepts of villages and towns to Basic Imperial Law to the Taboo Index and even to personal oaths sworn to the gods.

The higher up in the ruling structures one was, the fewer number of laws that applied, but even Cardinal and Administrator, the very highest of managers in this system, were still subject to them. The range of activities that their parents had limited them to in their youth was still active. Hence, Cardinal couldn't put her teacup directly on the table, and Administrator couldn't kill human beings.

But Administrator had just proven to me in person that she was no longer bound by her own oaths to her gods. It was clear evidence that she did not have a shred of belief in Stacia, Solus, or Terraria, the three goddesses at the center of the Axiom Church's influence.

Naturally, Chudelkin was unable to see through his master's deception. He heard what she said, her words dripping with derision, and his eyes filled once again with bulging tears.

"Oh...ohhh...I am filled...I am enshrouded in limitless joy...In this moment, I am supremely enabled, sublimely motivated...In short, I am *unstoppable*!!"

His tears sizzled and evaporated, and suddenly Chudelkin's entire body was glowing a furious, flaming red color.

"Sys! Tem! Caaaall!! Generate...Therrrmaaal...Elemennnnn-nntoah!!"

His limbs sliced the air, fully extended and straight, down to the fingertips, at the ends of which appeared a multitude of burning red dots. From my position standing behind Alice, I could keenly sense that this was Chudelkin's last and greatest attack.

Like the ice, the number of glittering ruby heat elements was twenty in total. Chudelkin's balancing entirely on his head meant that his legs no longer had to support his body. But clearly, having the strength of mind and imagination to separately envision and control all ten toes in addition to his fingers required great practice.

While his eccentric appearance and personality drew all the attention, Prime Senator Chudelkin clearly had as much training as the oldest of the Integrity Knights—if not more—and was a tremendous foe in his own right.

His eyes narrowed in a gloating manner, as if he sensed my fear—and then they bulged as far as they could. His tiny pupils shone with red light, turning my fear into shock. At first, I almost thought he was like a classic heroic protagonist whose blood burned so passionately that his eyes turned into literal flames… but then I realized my mistake.

The "flames" I saw burning right in front of Chudelkin's eyes were actually large heat elements. He could use even his own two eyes as control vectors…They were the twenty-first and twenty-second elements under his control.

Before being expended, the elements in waiting did release a small amount of their resources into the nearby air. Having heat elements an inch or two away from your fingertips caused a bit of a prickling sensation, but I could tell that having larger elements so very close to one's eyeballs couldn't be safe. Soon the skin around his eyes was fizzling and charring.

But the prime senator didn't seem to feel any heat or pain. With his eye sockets blackening, his strange face looked downright demonic. He grinned wickedly and screamed in ear-piercing falsetto, "Witness, my greatest of sacred aaaaaarts…Come forth, genie, and burn these rebels into ash!!"

He pulled his limbs in, then swung them about with blinding speed. The twenty elements didn't change form immediately but flew into the air in parallel lines of five each, hurtling through the space between him and us with startling velocity.

To my stunned disbelief, the glowing red lines came together to depict a very large human. It had short legs. A bulging gut. Oddly long arms. And a head wearing a crown with several spikes on it. It was an enormous clown, as if Chudelkin's original puffed-up form had grown to several times its size.

The last of the elements filled in the crimson stripes that made up the suit of the twenty-foot-tall burning clown, and then they vanished. Its face, which was so high I had to crane my neck to see it, was based on Chudelkin's features but looked many times more cruel. A tongue of flames licked out of its heavy lips, and the fissures that represented its eyes exuded a gaze that was paradoxically freezing cold.

Now that he was done waving his limbs around to create the flaming clown, Chudelkin at last closed his eyes so hard it was audible. The last two heat elements shot forth and took hold in the dark sockets of the clown to form burning red eyes.

The enormous clown glared at us with horrifying malice—it was as though Chudelkin's very soul had transferred to it. It lifted the pointed boot of its right foot and pressed it down on the ground in front of it. The floor rumbled, and a great billow of flame erupted from the giant's foot, singeing and hazing the air around it.

Eugeo and I were stunned into silence during the entire display. It wasn't until Alice's interjection that we snapped out of it and brandished our swords once more.

"…I'll admit that I did not know he was capable of such a thing," she whispered. Her words were as precise and controlled as ever, but I didn't miss the slight wobbliness in her voice. "It seems we misread Chudelkin. Sadly, my flowers cannot destroy that bodiless flame giant. Even on defense, they will not withstand a direct attack for long."

"…Meaning that in the meantime, we'll have to do the job of attacking Chudelkin's actual body," I whispered hoarsely.

"Precisely right," Alice returned. "I'll find a way to block him for ten seconds. Kirito, Eugeo, you must find a way to vanquish Chudelkin in that time. But you cannot approach within sword-strike range. That is what the pontifex is waiting for."

"Ten..."

"...seconds."

Eugeo and I shared a look and groaned.

When we'd fought on the floor below, Eugeo had overpowered me with his icy impassiveness, but after his knighthood had been undone, he'd gotten his emotions back. Oddly enough, the sight of fear and hesitation in his face made me a bit happy. It was reassuring.

But this was time to think. If Alice just wanted us to rush Chudelkin while she handled the fire clown, we had several options. I'd taken on that role many times against floor bosses in Aincrad, and Chudelkin ought to be defenseless while he was controlling the clown.

On the other hand, there was no guarantee that Administrator would stay still and watch while we charged. So we had to keep our distance as we attacked. Being swordsmen, there were only two ways for us to attack from a distance.

One was using sacred arts. But with the level of arts that Eugeo and I were capable of casting, I couldn't imagine that we could break through Chudelkin's defenses to actually do serious damage to his life.

The other was the ace up our sleeve, Perfect Weapon Control— but this had a weakness. Activating it demanded the chanting of the extremely long command that Cardinal put together for us. It would take well over ten seconds. As an Integrity Knight, Eugeo had used Perfect Control without a vocal command, but I didn't think he could do it again now. I certainly couldn't.

"...!"

I ground my teeth in frustration. The burning clown moved forward mockingly, its body swaying and wavering in the heat. The movement was far from agile, but its size was all that mattered. Each step brought it several feet closer.

Once it was close enough that I could feel the heat radiating against my skin, Alice moved at last. She swung the Osmanthus Blade high overhead. Her free left hand was straight backward, and her legs were wide apart front and back, as tense as bowstrings.

A whirlwind gust erupted at Alice's feet, fluttering her long white skirt and golden hair. The Osmanthus Blade shone with golden light and split into hundreds of petals that began to glide through the air in a line.

"Spin, my flowers!!" she shouted, so loud I had to wonder how her body could produce such a sound.

The golden petals swirled at such a high speed that they became individually invisible, melting into a blur that grew into a huge tornado.

When grinding the ice cube, she'd created a cone with a sharp, focused point, but this was now the reverse. It was like a funnel that grew into the air at a diagonal from Alice's hand, over fifteen feet across at the widest end. The rotating golden storm sucked in the air around it, sending out random gusts that buffeted my body and Eugeo's.

The flame clown was so close it could practically flatten us. Smirking all the while, it launched itself into a jump nearly to the ceiling and came down fearlessly into the middle of Alice's tornado. There was a sizzling sound like a furnace bubbling away, so loud that it drowned out all other sound.

The fire clown's feet were swallowed up in the nearly vertical golden tornado. Ripped apart by the rapidly spinning blades, the flame burst apart in all directions like sparks, singeing the air.

But the clown maintained its enormous size, still holding that hideous smile that stretched from one side of its face to the other. Ever so slowly, it began to stomp on the tornado. Directly underneath, Alice's legs were trembling, and there was ferocious concentration on what I could see of her face.

The tiny petals began to take on the heat, turning red from the clown's powerful flame. Even now, Alice and her Osmanthus Blade were undoubtedly taking steady, solid life damage.

Eight seconds left.

It was impossible to defeat Chudelkin with sacred arts. There wasn't enough time for Perfect Control. The only things I had on my side were the black sword in my hand and the techniques that were fully committed to muscle memory.

During the two years I'd spent here, I'd practiced and repracticed countless sword skills so that I could teach Eugeo all about the Aincrad style. In the process, I'd realized that in this world, sword skills could sometimes exhibit a power that far surpassed their original specs in the game of *SAO*.

That was because in the Underworld, much of the outcome of actions was determined not by system calculation but by the strength of the user's will and imagination. The little spider named Charlotte and Alice the Integrity Knight had called this power Incarnation.

In other words, here, the power and range of sword skills that were strictly defined in the old Aincrad might actually be augmented by the power of Incarnation.

But on the other hand, it also meant that negative emotions like fear, timidity, and hesitation could weaken the same skills.

There was a strong, fundamental desire within me to distance myself from the Kirito avatar I had cultivated in the *SAO* days: the Black Swordsman and the Dual Blades master. I wasn't able to analyze the precise cause of that feeling. Maybe it was a desire not to be treated like a hero. Maybe it was guilt over those people whose lives I'd failed to save or ended. Either one could be true, but it might also have been something completely different that I had yet to figure out.

All I knew for certain was that no matter how much I might dislike it, Kirito the Black Swordsman was a part of me, had helped shape who I was now, and was giving me strength.

The same man who'd fought in that world—the same *me*—was still here.

Seven seconds left.

With the heat of the giant stomping on Alice's tornado plastering my cheeks, I turned my stance to the right and lowered my waist.

I lifted the black sword to the level of my shoulder, laid it perfectly flat, and pulled back.

My left hand provided catapulting leverage.

I hadn't used this skill or taught it to Eugeo or even attempted re-creating it yet. And I knew why: Because this sword skill was the one the Black Swordsman knew best of all and used the most often. It was his symbol.

On a straight line from the end of the slightly translucent black sword and about fifty feet away was the upside-down Prime Senator Chudelkin. His seared eyes were still closed, but he was obviously using some means of sharing the sight of his flaming clown. He should have noticed my motion already.

There would be only one shot at an attack. I couldn't let him defend or evade it. In that sense, fifty feet was such a tremendously long distance. Balancing on his head meant Chudelkin couldn't move quickly, but I'd already seen plenty of the little clown's resilience in a pinch. I needed his attention diverted away from me, if just for a quarter of a second.

Six seconds left. With as few words as possible, I whispered to my partner, "His eye."

"Got it."

His response was so immediate, so primed to go, that I glanced at him and saw that there was now a shining arrow of ice in Eugeo's right hand. It wasn't all that big, but the brilliance of its light was a sign that it had a high system priority. I supposed he must have taken the ice resources in the air from Alice and Chudelkin's fierce battle and converted them for use without anyone noticing.

Five seconds left. Eugeo moved his hands as though pulling on a greatbow, and the arrow in his grasp flashed blue.

"Discharge!!"

With that, the arrow of ice flew, but not straight at Chudelkin. Eugeo's left hand guided it in the air, first around the right of the flame clown, then curving left and upward. With all the red from the flames filling the chamber, the blue trail the ice arrow left behind stood out by contrast. The clown's burning eyes followed its course.

Four seconds left. When the ice arrow had nearly reached the domed ceiling, Eugeo clenched his controlling hand. On command, the arrow plunged at twice the previous speed. Its vicious head bore down—and not on Prime Senator Chudelkin.

But on Administrator, who lay prone in the air behind him.

Three seconds left.

The silver-haired woman showed no signs of alarm at Eugeo's brilliant ice attack. She merely glanced upward in annoyance, puckered her lips, and blew out a little puff of air.

That was all she did. But the arrow of ice promptly melted, several feet away from her.

The true attack Eugeo was making was not on Administrator herself, however, but on Chudelkin's abnormal fixation and attention on her. The instant the arrow flew behind him, Chudelkin's eyes bulged, and he rotated around on his head.

"Your Holiness, bewaaaare!"

Two seconds left.

I was already on the move before Chudelkin's scream hit my ears. I held the sword at shoulder height, right arm pulled back as far as it could go. The preliminary motion kicked in and turned the blade red as blood.

The system started moving my body automatically. My feet, wide apart, launched off the floor. The acceleration was funneled into my rotation, traveling through my back into my right shoulder. The rotation went back into a straight motion, bursting through my right arm into the sword that was now just an extension of it.

With the metallic roar of a jet engine, the sword burst forth in a straight line with a shining crimson light that was deeper than any of the flames.

This was the One-Handed Sword skill Vorpal Strike.

The reason I had used this skill so much in *SAO* was because it had the tremendous power to change the course of any battle, and a range that seemed almost unfair for a One-Handed Sword attack. The crimson effect carved through a space about twice the length of the blade itself. When combined with the full reach of my arm, it could sometimes outdistance even a long spear.

But the distance to my target, Prime Senator Chudelkin, was a good fifty feet. A normal Vorpal Strike would never reach him.

In other words, I had to use my imagination—my Incarnation power—to extend my first use of this attack in the Underworld to over five times its range.

This would not be easy.

But I didn't think it impossible. I would never think it.

Alice was exposing herself and her blade to hellfire, trusting in me to find the solution. My best friend, Eugeo, had used all his smarts and concentration to unleash a sacred art that would allow me this opportunity.

If I couldn't step up and do my part for them, I had no right to call myself a swordsman.

And I was nothing if not Kirito the Black Swordsman.

"Rrraaaahhh!!" I bellowed, summoning all my force. At that moment, a fingerless black glove covered my right hand, as though it had seeped out of the very air around me.

On its heels, smooth black leather appeared over my battle-torn sleeves, stretching up my arms to my shoulders, then my torso. Instantly, it turned into a long coat, the studded hem whipping wildly.

The light effects around my sword flashed brighter, almost like an explosion. From one concentrated point at the tip of the sword, they practically drowned out the red light coming from the flaming clown.

"Aaaah!!"

I unleashed all the power at my disposal.

One second left.

2

What was that sound?!

Eugeo gaped at the abnormal roar coming from just nearby.

All ultimate techniques created a multitude of lights and sounds. But this was different from anything he'd heard to this point. It was thicker, heavier, harder, sharper—just like the sword was roaring on its own.

The sound was coming from the black sword in Kirito's right hand. It sparkled like black crystal, the blade's sharp edge rattling and emitting an ear-splitting roar. And it wasn't just sound—the entire sword was wreathed in deep-red light.

It's a special technique. But I've never seen this kind before.

Eugeo held his breath. But the truly shocking part of this was what happened right after that.

This time, his partner's entire body flashed brightly and transformed into an appearance that he'd never worn before.

Kirito had been dressed in a black shirt and pants, tattered somewhat from all the fighting they'd done. But after the wave of light passed over his arm, body, and legs, a long, dark leather cloak with a high collar and a pair of slim-fitting leather trousers appeared out of nowhere.

That happened in less than a blink, but the strange phenomenon did not end there. There were more changes to Kirito's body, though they weren't as dramatic as the changes to his clothes.

First, his black hair was longer now, covering half of his profile. Also, what was visible of his eyes through the wild blowing of his bangs was fiercer than anything Eugeo had seen before. They were wild, the look harder—harder than when they'd fought the goblins in the northern cave, harder than when he'd cut off Raios Antinous's arms, harder even than when he'd fought against Deusolbert and Fanatio. It was like Kirito's very spirit had fused with the sword, becoming sharper and more dangerous.

His lips peeled back to expose his canines as he growled, "Rraaaaahh!!"

Kirito's sword also blazed with metallic sheen, the red light rapidly increased in intensity, and then his friend's hand shot forward with blinding speed. The long hem of his coat flapped behind him like monstrous wings.

It was clear that this was an ultimate technique of the Aincrad style.

But what a tremendous thrust it was. It was unlike any of the moves he'd learned from Kirito; its ferocity seemed more High Norkia in style but with all the ornamentation and beauty removed. It was an attack meant for nothing but piercing a target...

"......!"

Eugeo sucked in a breath and followed the crimson shine with his eyes.

Kirito was aiming, of course, for Prime Senator Chudelkin, who was controlling the fiery behemoth. But the target was at least fifteen mels away. No special technique would reach that far as long as it was from a sword.

The moment Kirito unleashed the thrust, Chudelkin wasn't watching him. He was gazing toward the rear of the room, where Eugeo had shot his ice arrow just seconds earlier.

Eugeo had used all his knowledge and creativity to attempt that trick, but of course it didn't work on Administrator, who

simply shattered it with a breath. But as Eugeo expected, Chudel-kin couldn't possibly ignore an attack on his master and had to turn to shriek a warning. As Kirito had requested, he'd managed to distract their target.

Relieved that the ice arrow had vanished without a threat, Chudelkin turned back, still on his head. Instantly, his narrow eyes fully opened, revealing a quick succession of emotions.

First was shock upon registering the sound and light of Kirito's oncoming sword.

Second was relief upon recognition that it was a thrust that surely wouldn't reach him.

Lastly, he felt terror at the realization that the red light causing all that metallic roaring was still coming closer.

Like him, Eugeo was too surprised to breathe. The bloodred light passed by Alice, who was still blocking the atronach, and jumped through all fifteen mels in an instant—until it easily shot right through the upside-down Chudelkin's stick-thin torso.

The blade of light extended nearly another two mels, then dissolved into little points of deep-red light that hung in the air like motes.

And then a gushing jet of actual blood shot through the air.

It was coming from a massive hole in the center of Chudelkin's chest, nearly large enough to bisect his body.

"Oh-hooooooo…" He exhaled weakly, like air escaping a balloon. His body slowly tilted until he toppled with a splat into a puddle of his own blood.

It continued gushing out, a seemingly impossible amount for such a small form. Chudelkin lifted a trembling arm, reaching for the floating Administrator.

"…Y…Your…Hol…i…ness…"

Eugeo couldn't see the little man's expression from where he stood.

But Prime Senator Chudelkin's hand fell to the soggy carpet with a squelch, and he moved no more.

At the same moment, the clown of flames that had been just

about to crunch through Alice's golden tornado vanished, its puffed-up torso evaporating into smoke, briefly leaving that evil grin before it too disappeared. As though baffled by the loss of their enemy, Alice's little golden blades slowed until they hung in the air.

Eugeo felt his ears ringing in the sudden and complete silence that fell over the room. He glanced to his right. Kirito was paused in a low crouch, his right arm extended as far as it could go.

The light that covered the black sword's surface vanished, and the tail of his coat flapped once more before it hung still. Right before Eugeo's unbelieving eyes, Kirito's appearance went hazy and changed back to the way it had been before.

Kirito still didn't move after he was back in his simple black shirt and pants. Eventually, he let his right arm drop until the tip of the black sword landed on the carpet, and he hung his head.

Eugeo didn't know what to say to him.

Kirito had tried to save even Vice Commander Fanatio. Even against someone like Prime Senator Chudelkin, he would never celebrate the taking of another's life. With his bangs back to being short, it was easy to see that the icy harshness he'd shown in the moment of his attack was gone.

Only the sharp ringing of Alice's cloud of golden petals clicking back into their rightful place broke the silence, several seconds later. Sensing a hint of nervousness in her demeanor, Eugeo looked over her shoulder toward the other end of the room.

Administrator, floating in the air, was reaching out her delicate hand toward the collapsed prime senator.

It was obvious from a glance that Chudelkin was dead. She couldn't possibly be administering healing arts. Or did she actually have the ability to bring corpses back to life…?

Eugeo sucked in a sharp breath, right as the pontifex's utterly impassive voice said, "I'm only cleaning him up, because it's such an unsightly mess."

She waved her hand lazily, and Chudelkin's body flew into the air as easily as if it were made of paper, slammed into the window on the distant eastern side of the room, and fell into a little heap there.

"...How could you...?" Alice murmured under her breath.

She was still the cold, dispassionate Integrity Knight whose personality had been tinkered with, but even Eugeo understood why she felt the need to speak up. Chudelkin was hardly respectable, but at the very least, he had given his life fighting for the sake of his master. The least he deserved was a worthy burial for his remains.

But Administrator didn't spare a second glance for his corpse. If anything, the way she was smiling mysteriously made it seem like she'd completely wiped all knowledge of the prime senator from her mind already.

"...Well, that was a very tiresome show," she said, "but I suppose I did glean a little bit of meaningful data from it."

Her voice was innocent and beautiful, and she even threw in a few sacred words that Eugeo did not recognize. Without breaking the sideways pose atop her invisible couch, she slid five mels through the air, into the center of the round chamber.

Administrator pulled back a lock of silver hair that had fallen over her face in the wind, then narrowed her reflective rainbow eyes and placed that magnetic stare right next to Eugeo—onto Kirito, who was still crouched.

"Irregular boy. I had thought my inability to read your properties was because you were an unregistered unit from an unofficial marriage...but that's not the case. Did you come from over there? Are you one of the people...from the *other side*?"

Eugeo hardly understood the implication of anything that she whispered.

Over there? The other side...?

Kirito, his black-haired partner, had appeared without any of his memory in the forest south of Rulid two and a half years ago, a so-called Lost Child of Vecta.

The town elders had told Eugeo that such people sometimes appeared. But it was only when he was a little child that he'd actually believed Vecta, the god of darkness, was reaching over the End Mountains to play tricks on the memories of people, the way the stories said.

When people experienced things that were tremendously sad and painful, they could actually lose their memories and sometimes even their lives. Eugeo had learned that from Old Man Garitta, the previous carver of the Gigas Cedar. Years ago, Garitta's wife had drowned, and his grief had been so great and so deep that he'd lost over half of the memories of his life with her. He had chuckled sadly and told Eugeo that this was both the mercy and the punishment of Stacia, goddess of creation, at work.

So Eugeo had always secretly assumed that this must be what had happened to Kirito, too. He would've been from the eastern or southern empire, based on the color of his hair and eyes. Something horrible and sad had happened to him back home, and he'd wandered for a long time without memory, until he'd eventually come to the forest near Rulid.

This was partially why Eugeo hardly ever brought up the topic of Kirito's past while they were on their long journey to Centoria and through the academy. Of course, there was also the fact that he was scared Kirito might remember and then go back to his real home, never to return.

However, Administrator, who had the power to see all things that happened in the human world, had used a strange term to describe Kirito's origin.

The other side. Did she mean the other side of the End Mountains, in the Dark Territory? Was the one clue to Kirito's birth, his consecutive-attacking Aincrad style of swordfighting, actually a school developed in the land of darkness?

No. She would certainly have more knowledge of the Dark Territory than that. The Integrity Knights under her control ranged freely over the mountains to do battle with the dark knights there. It was impossible to imagine that Administrator, the supreme ruler, would not know what the Dark Territory was like, how its towns looked, and what kinds of lives the residents lived there. She wouldn't need to use a vague placeholder term like *the other side.*

Which would mean…

Administrator was referring to something even she couldn't see, some place outside of the very world…? Something beyond even the Dark Territory…or perhaps even farther, even more removed. Like some kind of other world entirely…?

This concept was so abstract for Eugeo that he couldn't even find the words to describe the thoughts in his head. But his hunch told him that he was on the verge of something unbelievably massive, some kind of great secret of the entire world. Unable to resist a sudden burning impatience, he looked around, out the huge windows, into the night sky.

Between the black shapes of the clouds was a sea of stardust.

Was Kirito's home…somewhere on the other side of the sky? What kind of place was it? And did Kirito in fact have those memories back now…?

Several seconds of silence were eventually broken by his black-haired partner. Kirito got to his feet and answered Administrator's question with a simple and monumental "Yes."

Eugeo stared at his partner, feeling himself go numb with shock. Kirito *had* gotten his memory back already.

In fact…had he *always* had his memory, right from the start…?

For an instant, Kirito looked back at Eugeo. There was a multitude of emotions in his black pupils, but it seemed to Eugeo that foremost among them was pleading, a desperate wish for Eugeo to trust him.

Then he looked back at Administrator. Despite the fierce determination on his features, there was also a note of self-deprecation. He held out his hands and said, "But…my designated authority level is the same as any other person in this world, and far from your own, Administrator…or should I say, Quinella?"

The instant he said that mysterious-sounding name, the grin vanished from the pontifex's beautiful features. It was only for an instant, however, and soon a much larger smile was playing on her luscious lips.

"So I see the little one in the library has been filling your head with silly tales. And...? What did you come tumbling into my world to do? And without any kind of administrative privileges."

"I may not have privileges, but I do know some things."

"Oh? Such as? Be warned, I have no patience for old, foolish tales."

"Then how about the future?" Kirito offered, sticking the point of his sword into the floor and resting both hands on the pommel. There was harsh tension in his cheeks again, along with a fiery look in his black eyes. "In the fairly near future, Quinella, you are going to destroy your own world."

All this shocking pronouncement achieved was to deepen the smile on Administrator's face.

"...I will? It's not the boy who tormented so many of my sweet little puppets who will destroy the world, but *me*?"

"You heard me. And your mistake was that you created the Integrity Knights to fight off an all-out invasion from the Dark Territory. Their existence is the mistake."

"Hah. Ha-ha-ha-ha."

It was almost certainly the first time, at least since she became the supreme ruler, that Administrator had ever been corrected by someone else. She put her finger to her lips, and her shoulders shook, as if she was holding in a gale of laughter.

"Hee-hee-hee. Yes, that *does* sound like something she'd say. She must have practiced her feminine wiles, if she was able to ensnare boys like you with that childish appearance. I merely feel pity...both for her jealous desperation to see me fall and for you willingly being her cat's-paw." She chuckled deep in her throat.

Kirito opened his mouth to say something, but a different voice spoke up first, loud and determined.

"Forgive my interruption, Pontifex."

It was Alice the Integrity Knight, who had been silent all this time, now striding forward in her metal armor. Her long blond hair shone brilliantly in the moonlight, as if competing against Administrator's own silver locks.

"It was also Commander Bercouli and Vice Commander Fanatio's view that the Integrity Knights at present would not be sufficient to fight back the coming invasion of the forces of darkness. And mine, as well. Of course, every last member of the knighthood would fight to the bitter end if need be, but do you have a means to protect the defenseless citizens after the Integrity Knights are all gone? Surely you cannot be thinking that you alone could destroy all of the enemy's hordes!"

Her fierce, beautiful voice swept through the chamber like a cool breeze, ruffling her adversary's hair. The pontifex's smile waned. She stared at her knight in gold, seemingly surprised.

Alice's words came as a shock to Eugeo, too, for a different reason.

Alice Synthesis Thirty the Integrity Knight. The temporary, artificial persona that now inhabited the body of his childhood friend Alice Zuberg.

She was a cold and impartial administer of the law's justice—or should have been, the way that she had smacked Eugeo when she'd arrested them at the academy days ago. Within Alice the Integrity Knight, there shouldn't have been a single smidgen of all the emotions that made Alice who she was—her kindness, her innocence, her love.

But the way she had just spoken was different. It was as if the old Alice had grown into being an Integrity Knight herself.

She didn't notice the way Eugeo was gaping at her. The Integrity Knight thrust the end of the Osmanthus Blade into the floor with a mighty *clang!* and continued, "Holy Pontifex, earlier I said that your obsession and deceit brought the knights to ruin. Your obsession was in the way that you stole all weapons and power from the people of the realm, and your deceit lies in how you even abused your faithful Integrity Knights! You tore us away from our parents—from wives and husbands and siblings—locked away our memories, and filled us with false pasts, telling us we were summoned from some celestial realm that does not exist..."

She stopped, lowering her gaze momentarily, then straightened up and defiantly continued, "If this was a necessary thing to protect this world and its people, I will not chasten you at this moment. But why could you not even trust in the loyalty and respect we have for you and the Axiom Church?! Why did you have to implement such accursed measures that forced our very souls into servitude?!"

Eugeo saw a number of tiny droplets slide down the profile of Alice's shapely face.

Tears.

Tears, from Alice the Integrity Knight, who should have lost all emotion.

As he watched, stunned, the knight arched her back to stare boldly up at her ruler, without bothering to wipe her cheeks clean.

But those words, sharper than any sword, failed to register on Administrator any more than a slight breeze would. She smiled coldly and said, "Well, well, Alice. These are quite heady thoughts you've been juggling. And it's only been five...six years? So little time...since I created you."

Her tone of voice was the lightness that came from the lack of any emotion or connection. It was also reminiscent of polished silver. There wasn't even the barest hint of warmth in it.

"...You claim that I did not trust in my Integrator units? Why, I'm almost offended. I trusted you very much...You were my sweet little clockwork puppets, rattling away for my benefit. You clean and polish your sword regularly so it doesn't get rusty, don't you, Alice? It's the same thing. The Piety Modules I gave you are my present, the proof of my love. That way, you can always be my sweet little toys. You won't be plagued by all the stupid troubles and pains that the lower people have."

And with that transcendent smile, Administrator lifted her left hand and spun the triangular prism between her fingertips. It was the improved version of the Piety Module she'd taken from Eugeo's forehead.

Through its wavering purple light, she gazed down at Alice and whispered, "Poor, poor Alice. Look at how your pretty face is twisted. Are you sad? Or are you angry? If you'd just stayed as my little puppet, you would never, ever have had to feel such point-less things."

Alice's tears dripped lightly off her cheeks to hit her golden metal armor, a sound that was joined by something hard creak-ing. It was the Osmanthus Blade pointed into the ground at her feet—and piercing the thick carpet to gouge right into the marble floor underneath.

She clenched the sword so hard she was damaging the inde-structible structure of Central Cathedral, her voice cracking and trembling. "So you think that Uncle...Commander Bercouli spent three hundred long years of service to you without the slightest bit of anguish or doubt? You are saying you don't recog-nize the long-held pain within the heart of the man who swore deeper, longer loyalty to you than anyone else did?"

There was an especially loud crack from the sword. Alice drowned it out by bellowing, "Sir Bercouli was constantly torn between his loyalty to the Axiom Church and his duty to pro-tect the common people! Many times he pleaded to the senate to strengthen the Royal Knights of the four empires, who were knights in nothing but name, but I don't suppose you knew that! He...Uncle even knew about the seal placed within our right eyes. That alone should be proof enough that he suffered a vast torment unlike anyone else's!!"

But even this ragged, tear-streaked missive was met by nothing but a cold smile on Administrator's pale features.

"...Why, this saddens me, to realize that you thought so little of my love. Of course I knew these things." She beamed, but there seemed to be a whiff of cruelty behind her expression. "My poor Alice, let me explain something to you. Number One...Bercouli did not start worrying about such tawdry things just now. In fact, he said much the same thing about a hundred years ago. So I fixed him."

She giggled musically. "I looked into Bercouli's memory, found the mass of troubles and anxieties, and erased the whole lot of them. And not just him...I do the same for any knight who's been around a good hundred years or so. I helped them forget all about the pain. Don't worry, Alice. I don't get bent out of shape over a little mischief. I'm going to erase whatever memory it is that's making you look so sad, too. You'll go back to being a precious little puppet with no need to think before you know it."

The only thing left in the cold, heavy silence that followed was Administrator's quiet, mirthless chuckle.

She wasn't human anymore.

It was so obvious to Eugeo now. The fresh wave of chills rolling over his skin told him as much.

She had the power to erase human memories or create them anew. Eugeo had undergone that terrifying process himself. Just a simple spoken command of three sacred words on his part was all it took for Administrator to lock his memories out of reach, make him into an Integrity Knight, and force him to attack Kirito.

If Administrator had gone through the full, proper process of the Synthesis Ritual, Eugeo probably wouldn't have regained his wits this way. But some hole in Eugeo's memories that had always been there—though he had no idea why or how—had ultimately saved him from that fate.

That didn't mean his sin was absolved. Against Chudelkin, all he was able to do was momentarily distract the enemy with sacred arts. He couldn't assume that alone made all forgiven. In truth, he still didn't have the right to stand side by side with Kirito...

He focused on the Blue Rose Sword clenched in his right hand, then felt Kirito's gaze on his cheek. But he couldn't look back and meet it.

Alice murmured, "Yes...I am feeling sadness and pain that

threatens to tear my breast asunder. It is a wonder that I even have the strength to stand."

Bit by bit, her trembling voice regained firmness. "But...I do not wish to erase this pain, this new sensation. It is the pain that tells me I am not just a knight puppet, but a real human being. Your Holiness, I do not wish for your love. I do not need you to fix me."

"...A puppet that refuses to be a puppet," Administrator replied musically. "But that does not make you human, Alice. Just a broken puppet. It doesn't matter what you think, I'm afraid. Once I resynthesize you, all of these feelings you have now, and everything else, will cease to exist," she said, the gentlest of smiles for the cruelest of words.

"Just like you did for yourself, Quinella," said Kirito, breaking his silence at last. Once again, he used that strange name. And once again, the smile vanished from the girl's face.

"Didn't I tell you not to bring up the past, little boy?"

"If I do, will that erase the truth? Even you can't alter the past as you please. You were born like any other person. You're a human being. And that fact can't ever be deleted...can it?"

Suddenly, it clicked into place for Eugeo. When they were in the Great Library, Kirito must have heard about Administrator's true name and birth from Cardinal.

"Human...yes. *Hu-man*," Administrator murmured sarcastically, the little grin back again. "I'll admit that hearing that word from a boy from the other side prompts some conflicting feelings. Are you saying you are more special than I am? That an Underworldian like me should shut up and mind my own business, perhaps?"

"Not at all," Kirito said, shrugging. "In fact, in many ways, I think the people from this world are superior to those on the other side. But at the root of it all, we're still the same human beings with the same souls. And you're no exception to the rule. Does living for a few hundred years mean a human being becomes a god? It doesn't, does it?"

"...And what is your point? That as human beings, we should all sit down and enjoy tea time together?"

"Well, I certainly wouldn't object to that...but my point is that because you're a human being, you cannot be perfect. People make mistakes. And the mistakes you've made are reaching the point where they cannot be contained. Now that the Integrity Knights are half ruined, if a full-scale invasion from the Dark Territory comes, the human realm will fall."

Kirito paused and glanced at Eugeo before continuing, "Eugeo and I were in the cave that goes through the End Mountains in the far north two years ago, and we fought a band of goblins that came from the far entrance. I'm sure whatever Integrity Knight was guarding the area must have missed them. That's going to happen far more regularly now. Eventually, the incursions will become an invasion, and the world you've taken such pains to maintain—or stagnate, as the case may be—will be exposed to an unstoppable wave of destruction and violence. I can't imagine that this is what you really want to happen."

"Says the boy who destroyed those knights himself. But your point is acknowledged. And?"

"You might think that as long as you survive, you can always start over afterward," he said, his tone getting harder and darker, as he slid his foot half a step forward. "Maybe you could create more laws to control the overflowing hordes of darkness and those lucky few human survivors—perhaps a new control structure, some Church of Darkness, or something along those lines. But unfortunately for you, that won't happen. Because on the other side, there are people who have true, absolute authority over this world. They're going to think this was a failure, and they can and will start over. With the push of a button, everything in this world will vanish. The mountains, the rivers, the towns...and all human beings, *including you*, will disappear in an instant."

By now, Kirito's words were beyond Eugeo's understanding. The same could be said of Alice. She turned, eyes red and puffy, looking at the black-haired swordsman with curiosity.

Only Administrator herself seemed to perfectly grasp the implications of whatever Kirito was saying. Her teasing smile was all but gone, replaced by narrowed silver eyes that seemed to freeze whatever they looked at.

"...No, that would not be pleasant," she said. "I do not like hearing that some stranger can treat this world like their own garden to do with as they please."

She steepled her slender fingers, covering the lower half of her face. The toying, teasing note in her voice when she'd been speaking to Alice was all but gone.

"But then...what of you? What of you people from the other side? Do you grapple at all times with the possibility that your world was created by some higher power and attempt to curry the favor of that force or being so that your own world is not wiped clean, too?"

Kirito did not appear to be expecting this question; he bit his lip and did not respond. Administrator sat up on the invisible floating sofa and spread her arms. Her long legs straightened out to a standing position. Her naked form was more beautiful than any depiction of a goddess, shining in the moonlight and casting an overwhelming holy presence throughout the room.

"...Of course you do not," she continued. "You people created a world and the lives within it, then decide to erase them when you do not care for them any longer. So, coming from such a world, what right do you have to argue with my choices, boy?"

She looked up at the ceiling—no, *through* the marble roof and into the night sky far beyond it—and declared, "I refuse. I will not beg those who fancy themselves gods of creation, pleading for the right to my continued existence. If you heard the tales the little ones recite, then you should know that my reason for existing is to rule, and nothing else. It is that desire alone that moves me and gives me life. My legs exist to climb over others to greater heights. They are not meant to bend at the knee!!"

The air rushed and swirled around her, buffeting her silver hair. Eugeo faltered a step, overwhelmed by the force of her presence.

Administrator was the enemy who overwrote Alice's memories and allowed the nobles to languish in corruption—but she was also the supreme ruler of the world, a being who was half human, half god, and would never spare a glance for a common peasant like him, a fact he was now reminded of.

Even the partner who had guided Eugeo all this way swayed with the weight of the moment, but then he recovered and took a step forward instead. He thrust his sword into the ground before him, just to emphasize his own presence.

"In that case," he bellowed, so loudly that the window behind him rattled, "are you going to let this land be overrun so that you can be the ruler of a nation without subjects, sitting on a throne in name alone, waiting for your lonely end?!"

All the youthful beauty of Administrator's carefully sculpted face melted away, and the full, true age of the woman underneath came to the fore in the form of pure rage. This too faded in short order, until her pearly lips wore that mocking smile again.

"...I'm offended that you think I haven't given a single thought to this all-out invasion, as you call it. I've had *plenty* of time to think...for time alone is my ally, and not the people on the other side."

"So you have some means of avoiding the end?"

"I have the means and also the objective. Ruling is my reason for existence...and there is no limit to its bounds."

"What...? What does that mean?" Kirito asked, taken aback. She didn't answer him immediately. Instead, she let a note of mystery linger in her smile, then clapped her hands together as if to say that the conversation was over.

"I can tell you the rest of it once you've become my puppet. And Alice and Eugeo, too, of course. But if you want a teaser, let me just add that I have no intention of accepting that the Underworld will be reset...or allowing the 'final stress test' to happen. I've already gotten a sacred art prepared for that. Rejoice, for you three will bear witness to it before anyone else."

"...Sacred art...?" Kirito repeated skeptically. "So you're going to rely on system commands and all their inherent limitations? You think that the commands you can execute will completely wipe out the hordes of darkness? When you can't even handle the three of us right here."

"Is that so?"

"It's true. Clearly, you have lost. Your long-range attacks will take seconds, and Alice can stop them. Meanwhile, Eugeo and I will cut you down. If you try to paralyze me with a contact-based command, I'll do what I just did to Chudelkin again. I hate to rely on theory at a time like this, but a single spellcaster without a front line to hide behind cannot beat a group of swordsmen. That's an ironclad rule that has to apply to this world, too."

"Single...single, you say," she chuckled. "That's a very good point. Yes, in the end, numbers are the problem. Having too many pawns means you cannot control them all. Too few, and they cannot withstand the stress test. I grew the Integrity Knights over time to meet that balance...but..."

Without her trusted retainer Chudelkin, the supreme ruler was all alone. But she exhibited boundless confidence in the face of the three rebels. "To tell you the truth, the knights were only a *stopgap*. The military force I truly seek doesn't need memory or emotion or even the power to think. All it needs to do is destroy whatever foe is before it, over and over. In other words...it doesn't need to be human."

"...What are you...saying...?" Kirito mumbled, but Administrator ignored him. She lifted her left hand high, holding the triangular prism that glowed an eerie purple color: Eugeo's Piety Module.

"He was an idiotic clown, but Chudelkin did prove himself useful. He gave me enough time to construct this drearily long command string. Now...awaken, my faithful servant! My soulless slaughterer!!"

That was when it hit Eugeo.

The sacred chanting he'd heard when he'd first returned to this room, coming from the inside of the bed. An extremely long art, one of the greatest challenges even for the pontifex, as it could not be abbreviated with willpower alone. And now she was about to execute it.

What she sang next was just two simple words, too brief to stop, but more horrifying than anything else she could have said.

"Release Recollection!!"

The ultimate form of Perfect Weapon Control. The true secret art that unlocked the weapon's unconscious memories and brought forth a power greater than any sacred arts...

But Administrator was completely naked, without so much as a knife on her person. It wasn't the Piety Module she was holding, was it? But that prism couldn't possibly have memories that could be released...

As he stared at the distant figure, Eugeo eventually became aware of a faint sound growing firmer. It was the metallic clinking of some object from behind...but now from the right and the left as well.

He spun around and moaned in shock at what he saw.

The forty-mel-wide chamber was supported by a number of pillars. And the gleaming golden swords in a variety of sizes that adorned those pillars were now trembling.

"Is...is this...?!" He gasped. Alice murmured, "It can't be...!"

The biggest swords were three mels long. Even Administrator couldn't possibly swing such a thing around. And from what Eugeo knew, the rumbling wasn't just coming from the one he was looking at. The same phenomenon was happening to all the pillars that lined the room. There were at least thirty of the swords in total.

But Memory Release was a skill that worked only on weapons that had been used so often, they might as well be a part of the wielder's body. It was through the deep relationship between master and blade that one could come into contact with the sword's memory at all.

The pontifex treated her own subjects like tools. There was no way she had such deep bonds with thirty different decorative swords. So what in the world was the "memory of the sword" she had just unlocked...?

As the three of them stood dumbfounded, there was an especially fierce rumble, and the enormous swords pulled away from the supports to float in the air. Eugeo had to duck as one swooped over his head, rotating madly. They gathered in the center of the room, right over Administrator. Then something even more shocking happened.

Thirty swords of various sizes rang loudly as they contacted one another, banging and sliding into place to form one gigantic mass. Eugeo noticed at once that it seemed to be vaguely humanoid in shape.

A thick backbone ran through the center, and long arms stretched to either side. There were legs below, but four of them instead of two.

When the swords finished transforming into the bizarre giant—no, *monster*—Administrator held out the Piety Module toward it.

That prism is the centerpiece of her Memory Release, Eugeo instantly sensed.

At the exact same moment, Kirito yelled, "Discharge!!"

Suddenly, there was a bird of flame in his outstretched right palm. While Eugeo—and likely Alice—had been watching the swords connect in shock, Kirito had busied himself with chanting an art.

The firebird shot forth toward the prism in Administrator's hand. There were many kinds of heat-based attack arts; the Bird Shape art that Kirito used automatically tracked its target. And the pontifex was concentrating on the sword giant above her, so she didn't notice Kirito. It was going to work! Eugeo was sure of it—

Until the next moment, when one of the sword giant's legs stretched out and blocked the bird's path. It was unable to dodge and smacked into the metal, bursting into deep-red droplets. The shining golden sword got a bit of soot on its surface but was otherwise unaffected.

Administrator completely ignored that whole sequence. She released the triangular prism in her left hand—not so much tossing it as letting the prism rise on its own until it fit inside the space between the three swords that formed the creature's backbone.

The purple light continued to rise until it came to a stop at about the spot a heart would be in a living being and flashed much brighter. That light then spread throughout the giant, and the swords that had seemed more decorative than practical suddenly rang loudly as their edges spontaneously sharpened. Eugeo's instinct told him that this was the completion of the pontifex's art.

Administrator narrowed her eyes and smiled.

Then the sword giant spread its four legs and leaped through the air in between the humans and the pontifex, landing on the floor with a thunderous rumble.

Eugeo gaped up at its towering five-mel height. Backbone, ribs, two arms, and four legs—all made up of golden swords. It was like a toy that a child would make out of carved branches... or some creature of living bone from the depths of the Dark Territory.

"...Impossible...," moaned Alice under her breath. "Controlling multiple weapons at once—thirty, at that—goes against the very properties of Perfect Control arts. It shouldn't be possible, even for the pontifex. She still has to follow the laws of sacred arts...So how is she...?"

Administrator would have heard her, of course, but the woman floating behind the sword giant ignored her. Instead, she gloated, "Ha-ha-ha...ah-ha-ha-ha-ha-ha. *This* is the power I sought. Pure attack, a power that will fight for eternity. Its name...will be Sword Golem, I have decided."

Eugeo tried to use what he knew about the sacred tongue to decipher the two strange words she had just said. He knew that the sacred word *Sword* came from weapon-enhancing arts. But he'd never even seen the word *Golem* in his textbook at the academy.

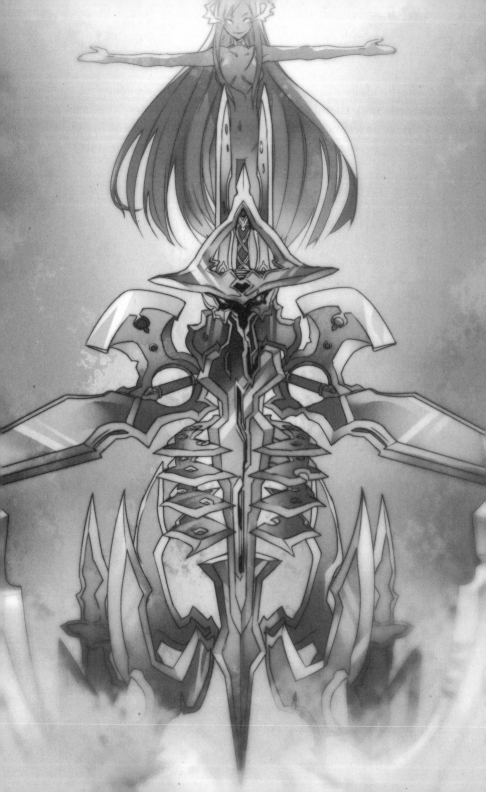

Alice didn't seem to know, either, and she would have a much stronger grasp of the terms.

The silence was broken by Kirito's hoarse mutter.

"A moving puppet...made of swords."

His description of it in the common tongue must have been correct; Administrator's smile widened, and she clapped her hands together.

"I should have realized that you would know your sacred language...excuse me, your 'Ing-lesh.' If you don't want to be a knight, I can still make you a secretary—but only if you drop your sword, apologize for your transgressions, and promise your eternal loyalty to me."

"Sadly, I have a hard time believing that you would trust my promise. Plus, I haven't given up on this one yet."

"I do not dislike this boldness of yours, but stupidity I cannot abide. Do you really think you can best my golem? Against a puppet whose each and every blade has the priority level of a Divine Object? The ultimate weapon of war, which I used every bit of my valuable memory space to construct...?"

Something about the term *ultimate weapon* stuck in Eugeo's mind. Yes, it reminded him of what Vice Commander Fanatio had said—that the pontifex used a thousand mirrors to gather Solus's light into a single point that could produce superheated flames without sacred arts. Fanatio had called it a "weapons experiment."

So a weapon of war would refer to some tool with more potential power than any sacred art. Was this Sword Golem standing before them now the realized form of just such a weapon...?

Whatever Administrator might have registered from the looks on their faces, she now waved her right hand with a cold, cruel smile on her lips. "Now...fight, my golem. Destroy your enemies."

And as though the giant had been waiting for just that command, its heart pulsed with purple light.

The four-legged monster issued a metallic roar and began to charge. Its size was not nearly as large as the clown of flames that

Chudelkin had created earlier. But the freakish way its many joints scraped and creaked as it approached froze Eugeo's heart with terror.

The golem swung its arms up high, each one made of three swords together. The quickest to react was Alice, who'd seemed paralyzed before this. Half a second after it moved, she was plunging forward, bravely meeting the monster's swing.

"Yaaaaaah!!" Her scream was even sharper than the golem's screeching. Her back arched as far as it could go as she wound up, clutching the Osmanthus Blade in both hands.

At that point, Kirito was moving, too. He leaped forward to his right, trying to circle around the golem. Eugeo was stock-still as of yet, too afraid to move, but he could at least attempt to discern what Kirito and Alice were doing.

They both suspected that if the golem had a weak point, it was where the backbone met its four legs—what would be the pelvis on a human. But it was too dangerous to attack the area head-on. So Alice was acting as a decoy to draw the golem's attention—if it was conscious enough to have such a thing—while Kirito tried to sever the weak point from the side. It was essentially the same strategy they'd used against Chudelkin.

Eugeo couldn't help but be impressed at how the two launched into this combined stratagem without any planning ahead of time. But there was a twinge of pain there, too.

Alice's sword traced an arc through the air as bright as Solus. The monster's right arm swung down ferociously. When the two golden blades connected, the resulting shock wave seemed to shake the entire cathedral, its wind buffeting Eugeo.

Just two seconds had passed since both sides charged.

And whatever you might call a "battle" ended at this exact moment.

Alice's Osmanthus Blade, a Divine Object with the property of "everlasting eternity," was easily overpowered by the golem's arm. The knight was unable to stop the backward momentum of her sword and lost her center of gravity.

As she struggled to regain her balance, the golem's left sword plunged in at blinding speed. Compared to the first rush, the little *thunk* that followed was barely noticeable. But it was the sound that heralded the end of the fight.

The ghastly huge tip of the sword appeared from Alice's back, spraying dark-red droplets. Her long, beautiful hair floated upward with the impact, taking the brunt of the spatter.

Her golden breastplate, which had been split clean in two, instantly shattered with the loss of its life value. The Osmanthus Blade fell from her hand and clattered on the ground.

Lastly, the golem promptly yanked its left arm back, leaving the Integrity Knight to fall to the floor.

"Aaaaaaahh!!"

It was practically a scream. That was Kirito, the black-haired swordsman just around the giant's right side, eyes livid with rage as he charged.

His black sword glowed a brilliant blue. That was the attack known as Vertical.

The golem would stop if they could shatter the Piety Module encased in its backbone, but it was heavily defended and too high for any ultimate techniques to reach. So Kirito was aiming at the point where the golem's spine met its legs instead. If just that point could be destroyed, it would prevent the giant from moving.

Just after its attack, with both arms lowered, the golem shouldn't have had a way to defend itself. But the moment Kirito's sword started to move, the giant's top half rotated around the spine with tremendous speed. It swung in a way that no human being could ever do, its left arm in a side swipe toward Kirito.

There was a blunt impact. With superhuman reflexes, Kirito changed the course of his technique and fought back the golem's strike.

But before Eugeo's horrified eyes, the exact same thing happened again.

Kirito rose off his feet, unable to bear the full brunt of the impact. The golem's back left leg promptly shot forward toward his unprotected side.

There was another heavy thud, and Kirito shot sideways until he crashed against an east-facing window. A frightening amount of blood splattered against the glass, and the swordsman in black crumpled to the floor.

Eugeo watched in silent shock as a pool of blood formed beneath his facedown partner; he could feel nothing in his own arms and legs. It was like his body didn't belong to him anymore. He was helpless to stop it from shivering.

Only his face was able to respond to commands. He turned it to look up at the Sword Golem standing just five or six mels away.

The monster looked straight back at him. The hilt of the sword located at the top of the backbone almost looked like a face. Two gemstones inlaid on the guard twinkled like blinking eyes.

He couldn't move or speak. All that Eugeo's numb mind was capable of doing was repeating the same thought.

It can't be.

It can't be. This can't be happening.

Alice and Kirito were essentially the greatest warriors in the entire world. They would never lose a fight together, even against a freakish creature—a weapon of war—like this one. They were going to get back up and draw their swords again, very soon…

Hee-hee. Hee-hee-hee.

Over the constant heavy grinding of the golem came a quiet chuckle. Eugeo saw then that Administrator, levitating in the background, was surveying the battle with great pleasure. The only color in her mirror eyes was the red of the blood that Kirito and Alice shed. There was not the tiniest bit of pity in them.

The giant creature began to move again, preparing to carry out its master's orders to completion. The front right leg raised and fell, taking a huge step. The front left leg followed it.

Red drops decorated the left arm of the approaching giant. Eugeo hoped it would just kill him and be done with it.

Even his fear was gone.

The entire world was utterly silent…

Until suddenly, a tiny voice popped into his head. So small, he didn't even realize he was hearing something at first.

"Use the dagger, Eugeo!"

It was a woman's voice, a bit deep but beautiful.

If this was an illusion just before his death, it certainly didn't sound like any voice from his past. He looked to his right and saw—

—resting on Kirito's right shoulder, barely the size of a human fingernail, a black spider.

But no bug that small could speak. Yet, there was something in the voice that made Eugeo believe it. Perhaps due to his exhausted wits, Eugeo fully trusted that the tiny creature, waving its front leg as if scolding him, was indeed the source of the voice in his head.

"I…I can't. The dagger won't reach her," he mumbled. The spider waved its raised leg even harder.

"No! The corridor! Stab the levitating disc in the floor!!"

"Huh…?"

His eyes went wide. The black spider stared back at him with its four little ruby eyes and said, *"I'll buy you time! Just hurry!!"*

Cute little fangs spun as the spider yelled at him. Then it turned briefly toward Kirito, who was looking pale, and brushed his cheek lightly with a single leg before jumping down to the floor.

The tiny black dot landed on the carpet without a sound.

Then it started running straight at the Sword Golem, a creature thousands upon thousands of times its size.

3

I thought I had a pretty good handle on physical pain.

A bit over two years ago, I had fought a group of goblins from the Dark Territory, in the cave to the north of Rulid. During that battle, the captain goblin's machete had caught my left shoulder, and though it hadn't been fatal, the agony had been so great that utter fear had paralyzed me and left me unable to react.

That experience was a huge wake-up call as to my physical weakness in the Underworld. I'd spent so long playing in worlds with the pain-absorption function of the NerveGear and AmuSphere that I didn't have any resistance to unrestricted physical pain.

Since then, I'd focused on keeping myself solid and tough when hit by wooden swords during practice with Eugeo or duels at the academy. Thanks to that, I was at least able to keep my wits and stop from freezing up when I suffered wounds when fighting the other Integrity Knights. And in the Underworld, anything was perfectly healable as long as your life didn't reach zero—even severed limbs.

But…right at the end of this long journey, I received a painful reminder that I hadn't actually conquered anything.

The power and speed of Administrator's battle weapon, the Sword Golem, were off the charts. It was impossibly capable, beyond the limits of what should have been possible in this world. Already it was miraculous that I was able to defend against the first blow from its arm, but I couldn't even see the one that had come from its leg.

The sword that made up its rear left leg entered my right flank and passed through to my left side, slicing everything in its path. The instant I first felt the shock, I recognized an icy chill brushing my belly, but after I'd been thrown against the window and I'd slumped to the floor, my insides were burning like they were on fire. I couldn't move a muscle. I didn't even have any sensation from my lower half. I could've been split in two with just a little scrap of skin holding me together, for all I knew.

In fact, it was a mystery as to how I could think at all.

Or perhaps it was just a sign that the despair was far more powerful than the actual pain assaulting me.

I knew my life had to be dropping at a calamitous rate. I didn't have more than a minute or two before it ran down to zero. And Alice had even less time than I did. The golden knight, now collapsed on the floor across the room, had been pierced through the chest. It hadn't hit her heart, from what I could tell, but the loss of blood would certainly do her in first. Perhaps even the highest level of sacred healing arts wouldn't help her now. Her miracle fluctlight, which had overcome the seal in the right eyeball that every Underworldian had, was about to perish before my very eyes.

Although I couldn't see him from my position, I was sure that my irreplaceable friend Eugeo's life was also hanging in the balance. His technical ability was greater than mine, but this was not a foe who could be handled with a blade.

Through foggy eyes, I saw the Sword Golem advance, shaking the ground. I wanted to shout at him to run, but the only thing my mouth could do was exhale weakly.

And even if I shouted, Eugeo wouldn't run away. He would raise the Blue Rose Sword and face this huge, unfair enemy to save his friends.

Worst of all, the cause of this horrible outcome was my own mistaken assumption: the idiotically naïve conjecture that Administrator couldn't kill human beings.

In the Great Library, Cardinal had used a teacup to demonstrate how the taboos of this world really worked. The point of her lecture was that all taboos had loopholes that could be exploited. Administrator had simply overcome hers not by acting on her own but by creating a weapon that would automatically kill her enemies for her.

The burning agony of my insides was starting to turn into an empty numbness. My life would fall to zero very soon. In that instant, my mind would be kicked out of this world, and I would wake up inside The Soul Translator. There, the Rath staffers would inform me that the current form of the Underworld—including all the fluctlights, like Alice and Eugeo—had just been wiped clean, deleted.

If only my life held the exact same meaning as Eugeo's and Alice's.

If only I could experience true death with them in this moment.

How else could I possibly apologize for what I'd put them through?

My vision was dimming now—the only things I could see were the legs of the advancing Sword Golem and the shining gold of Alice's hair on the ground. And even that light was waning.

That was when I heard a quiet but firm voice, right in my ear.

"Use the dagger, Eugeo!"

It was a smooth, silky tone that I was certain I'd heard before. But my mind was already too fuzzy to do anything with that information. The mezzo-soprano continued talking to my friend.

After it had delivered a few instructions, it said it would buy some time and moved away from my ear. For a moment, I thought I felt something warm touch my cheek.

That tiny little brush of warmth brought back some bodily feeling. I struggled to lift my half-closed lids.

Right before my eyes, a tiny, shining black spider landed on the bloodied carpet.

That was it. Charlotte. The very agent of Cardinal that had been hiding on my person for two whole years to gather information on me.

But why here? Why now? The spider had finished her duty when we reached the Great Library, and she had vanished into the cracks between the bookshelves.

I was so surprised by this that I forgot all the pain and terror. Before my eyes, the tiny creature sped toward the gigantic golem as it approached. Eight fragile legs buzzed along the carpet at dizzying speed. But each step for the spider was nothing compared to a step for the golem. How was she going to buy time for Eugeo to escape from the creature that was bearing down on him?

But in the next moment, I gasped weakly as a new shock came over me.

The spider's body got bigger.

With each contact of pointed leg against carpet, her body mass seemed to grow. First she was the size of a mouse, then a cat, then a dog, and still growing. Soon my ear, pressed against the carpet, could actually hear the vibration of each leg against the ground.

"*Greeeh!*" roared the Sword Golem—it had noticed Charlotte at last. The two gemstones on its "face" flickered, seemingly assessing this new enemy.

"*Shaaaa!*" hissed the spider, now over seven feet long, four eyes flashing menacingly.

She wasn't half as tall as the golem, but while the enemy was constructed entirely of long, narrow swords, the enlarged Charlotte's body was covered in thick, tough carapace. Wherever the light hit the black surface, it reflected in lustrous gold, and the claws on the ends of the eight legs were like obsidian.

The two front legs were especially large, their claws nearly as long as swords themselves. Charlotte raised the right one and smashed it against the golem's left leg.

A tremendous clanging filled the room, as though two greatswords had just collided. A shower of orange sparks lit up the darkened room.

And in that light, I was stunned to see the figure of Eugeo running. Not at the golem. Not for either me or Alice.

He was racing for the circular pattern in the carpet along the south wall, to carry out Charlotte's order to stab his dagger into the levitating platform.

Behind Eugeo, the Sword Golem lost its balance the tiniest bit after Charlotte's attack, but it promptly held firm, then raised its right arm high in the air to strike. The golem had identified the newly appeared spider as an enemy. Pale eyes glinting, it swung down its massive arm.

Charlotte lifted her front left leg to block it. The clash of golden sword and obsidian claw again resulted in a powerful vibration that made my body rattle at the edge of the room.

With the help of her six rear legs for resistance, the giant spider had succeeded at stopping one of the blows that had so easily knocked me and Alice off our feet.

The two giants held their limbs forth, each trying to push over the other. The hard carapace of Charlotte's legs warped under tremendous weight, and the joints of the three swords that made up the golem's right arm creaked.

The standoff lasted all of three seconds.

With a wet crunch, Charlotte's front left leg snapped off. Milky white liquid shot forth from the break over her black surface.

But the spider didn't stop. She swung her front right leg this time, right at the gap between the three greatswords that made up the Sword Golem's spine—toward the glowing purple Piety Module within.

Just when it seemed like the black lightning that was her claw would pierce the prism representing the golem's ultimate weak point, the many swords that formed the creature's ribs moved at once.

Like a paper cutter, the four blades on the left and the four blades on the right met in the middle.

Sha-shunk!! They easily sliced through Charlotte's leg, causing a fresh gush of her bodily fluid to spill forth.

The golem's ribs slowly parted, allowing the severed half of the leg to fall. Its gemstone eyes twinkled steadily, almost seeming to mock Charlotte over its impending victory.

But losing another one of her legs did nothing to diminish the spider's bravery. She hissed again and leaped toward her foe, thick mandibles churning for a bite.

Her attack did not land. The golem kicked upward with blinding speed, slicing off two more of Charlotte's left legs. The giant spider lost her balance and toppled to the floor.

Forget about it—run! I wanted to scream.

I'd never actually had a direct conversation with the spider named Charlotte. But she had always been with me, protecting me. When Raios and Humbert had torn up the zephilia flowers I'd been growing at the dorm, she'd even told me there was still a way to save them—when the only job Cardinal had asked her to do was simply keep tabs on me.

It wasn't right for her to die for this hopeless fight, just to buy us a little bit of time. I tried to yell for her to run, over and over, but nothing came out.

Somehow, Charlotte managed to stand with her four remaining legs, and she tensed for another mad charge at the golem. But its left arm was quicker, swinging down from overhead to stab deep into the black spider's curved abdomen.

"...Uhk..."

It was just the smallest gasp that finally escaped from my throat, far too weak to be the scream it was meant to be.

And just then, I saw nothing but purple light.

It was a shine I'd seen just once before. The band of light that shot around the room was one conglomeration of tiny script. It was the same light that had erupted when I'd used Cardinal's dagger to save the life of Vice Commander Fanatio.

Eugeo must have reached the platform and stabbed it with his own dagger. I wasn't sure what kind of result that would have, but at least I knew that he hadn't let the time Charlotte had bought with her suicidal charge go to waste.

When the light began to dim, the black spider was scrabbling at the floor with her remaining legs, trying to stand despite being impaled. Then the golem removed its sword with a wet *shlurk*, and her massive bulk fell limply into the white puddle below her.

Her four eyes had been as bright and brilliant as rubies before, but now they were losing their luster. They did catch sight of the levitating platform, and with blood dripping from her fangs, Charlotte whispered, "*Oh, good...He made it.*"

Her right legs trembled, rotating her body. Four eyes looked at me with tenderness.

"*I'm happy...that I got to fight with you...one...last...*"

Her words melted away into space. The round eyes flickered red and then went dark.

I felt my vision blur. Despite the fact that I myself was dying, my eyes brimmed with tears. The huge black spider began to shrink without a sound. The puddle of white liquid evaporated, too, leaving behind only a corpse about the size of my fingernail, rolled onto its back with four legs curled up above it.

The Sword Golem instantly lost all interest in the target once it had squashed the life from her, and it rotated until its gleaming eyes caught sight of Eugeo. The massive creature then turned its body ninety degrees, and its pointed legs thudded into the floor. It was heading for the waving ribbon of purple light.

With all the strength I had left, I raised my head a few inches and looked to the source of the light. On the southern end of the circular room, not that far from the window, there was a pulsating, glowing ring: the levitating platform that had brought Alice and me to the hundredth floor.

Something that looked like a tiny cross was stuck in the middle of the ring. That was the little bronze dagger, one of two that Cardinal had given me and Eugeo. She'd fashioned it from the magical resources in the braids that she'd been growing for two hundred years, and whatever the dagger pierced would open a channel through space directly to her.

It was meant to be the final weapon against Administrator, but on Charlotte's orders, Eugeo had stuck it into the platform on the floor. Now the entire thing was glowing purple. It rang and whined like a thousand tuning forks coming into harmony, until the very physical makeup of the dagger came undone, turning into a long pillar of light that ran between the circular platform and the ceiling.

Standing right next to it, Eugeo covered his face against the light with his arm. Even the Sword Golem came to a clanking stop, uncertain of how to respond to this unexpected phenomenon.

The pillar of light steadily expanded. At its center, a smooth dark-brown surface appeared—a board. But not any regular board. It was surrounded by a rectangular frame and had a silver knob on one side—it was a door.

As I had that moment of realization, the light flashed and disappeared. The high-pitched wavelength faded, and quiet returned to the chamber.

Something about the design and coloring of the thick door was familiar to me. Eugeo and I watched without a sound while the Sword Golem took a step forward, its programming active again.

Just then, there was a small, hard *click*, accompanied by an almost imperceptible shift in the air. The silver doorknob began to rotate. There was another click, and the door quietly began to open.

It was just a door standing in empty air, so once open, it should have just been the same room on the other side. But there was no moonlight shining through the space inside the open frame. It was completely dark.

The door continued its slow progress until it came to a stop when it was about a foot and a half open. The other side was still out of sight. The Sword Golem continued its forward advance, ignoring the door. In just three steps, it would have Eugeo within swinging range of its massive arms…Two steps…

Then the darkness beyond the door was full of light.

A pure-white lightning bolt shot horizontally out of the frame.

Grrrakow!! My ears were buffeted by a tremendous shock—one greater than any sacred art I'd ever witnessed. The bolt hit the Sword Golem head-on and wriggled like a living thing, turning the massive creature into a black silhouette.

It took several seconds for the thrashing lightning to finally die down. The Sword Golem, which seemed so hardy that it was unstoppable, slumped over and stopped moving. Its dozens of swords hissed and smoked, and the gemstone eyes blinked sporadically.

The monster stubbornly tried to move again, but another bolt from the doorway caught it. A sacred art of this power should require dozens of lines of sacred words, so this kind of rapid fire was astonishing. Scorched all over, the golem let out a high-pitched moan and tried to step back.

Just half a second later, the third and largest lightning bolt ripped past. This bolt, burlier and meaner than the prior two, tossed up the nearly twenty-foot battle creation as if it were made of paper. It spun through the air, passing to the right of the floating Administrator, and crashed to the floor on the other end of the room. The tremor of its fall seemed to shake the very foundation of Central Cathedral.

The upturned golem was immobile at last but not entirely dead. The tips of the swords that made up its limbs trembled and twitched. At the very least, it wouldn't be popping back up again anytime soon.

I looked back at the darkness through the doorway. I was already certain of the name of the person who would soon appear through it. Administrator was one of the two people in this world who could execute such rapid and transcendently powerful magic—and here was the other.

A thin staff and the small hand that held it were the first things to appear from the darkness. Next were a fragile wrist and a wide sleeve. A black velvet robe large enough to form several draping folds. A pointed hat with an ornament on it. A flat-soled shoe extended from the bottom of the robe to step silently onto the carpet.

The moonlight caught soft brown curls and small, silver-rimmed glasses. Large eyes that were young and yet filled with infinite wisdom glinted behind the lenses of the glasses.

Cardinal the sage, who was another incarnation of Administrator with equal powers, and who had spent an eternity isolated within her massive, hidden library, took several smooth steps forward in the moonlight before coming to a stop. The door closed on its own behind her.

How had Cardinal left the library, which existed in a space that was everywhere and nowhere, and come into this room? The key was the dagger that Eugeo had carried around, of course. On Charlotte's orders, he'd stabbed it into the levitating platform, causing it to be connected to Cardinal. That would have made it child's play for her to change the connecting point of the platform to the library.

The wise little sage wore the expression of a strict teacher as she stared at the top floor of the cathedral for the first time. Then she turned to Eugeo, who was standing right next to her, and gave him a quick nod. Next was Alice, still lying on the floor a short distance away. When her eyes met mine, she gave me a reassuring little smile and nodded once more.

Lastly, Cardinal arched her small back and stared up at Administrator, who was still silently floating on the far side of the room. Whatever emotion she was feeling about this showdown with her ultimate foe, their first meeting in two hundred years, I couldn't read from her profile.

Once she had taken stock of the situation, Cardinal raised the staff in her right hand. Her body rose off the ground, and she slid through the air to where Alice and I lay helpless on the ground.

She landed and brushed Alice's back with the head of the staff. Little glittering motes of light sprinkled down and sank into the knight's body.

Next, she tapped my shoulder with the narrow staff. Another warm shower of light appeared and engulfed my body, which was completely devoid of sensation by now.

The first thing that happened was that the cold, hollow sensation that filled me vanished, and the searing pain from the golem's attack to my abdomen rushed back to fill its place. I fought to keep from screaming, and the pain steadily melted into waves of warmth. As the agony subsided, my bodily sensations returned. I opened and closed my stiffened fist until I felt able to touch the wound on my torso.

The injury tingled sharply when I touched it, but to my shock, the gash that had nearly bisected my entire body was completely gone. In order to re-create that effect with healing arts, I'd have to sit in a sunny forest lush with resources, chanting for hours on end.

It was such a miracle that I had to fight the momentary urge to celebrate that I'd been saved—but I knew that such a miracle required an equal compensation. And not from me but from Cardinal. After all, this situation had to be exactly what Administrator wanted…

But Cardinal paid no heed to that horrifying possibility. She floated into the air again. When she landed this time, she was before the tiny black body that lay atop the carpet. With a little thump, she set the end of the staff against the ground. She took her hand off it, but the staff remained perfectly vertical on its own.

Cardinal crouched down and gently scooped the tiny body up off the carpet. She clutched Charlotte the spider to her chest, lowering her head, and in a voice too quiet to be fully audible, whispered, "You stubborn fool…I released you from duty, hailed your service, and told you to live the life you wanted in whatever bookshelf you desired."

Behind the round glasses, her long eyelashes blinked twice, then three times.

My right arm was finally able to move properly, so I reached out to grab my sword and used it as a crutch to get to my feet. I made my way unsteadily over to Cardinal and, ignoring all the things I should've said first, asked, "Cardinal…was that…Charlotte's true form…?"

The sage looked up, chestnut-brown curls bouncing and eyes misty. In her oddly old way of speaking, which almost seemed as nostalgic as if I hadn't heard it in ages myself, she said, "In this world...since ancient times, there have been many magical beasts and beings that made their homes in the forests and wilderness. I believe these creatures are familiar to you."

"...Named Monsters...But...Charlotte spoke human language and had emotions of her own...Did she have a fluctlight, too...?"

"No...To use the language of your world, she was the same as an NPC. She was not stored in a lightcube but was a tiny part of the Main Visualizer function, given a small simulated thought engine—in other words, a part of the system. In the past, there were many large animals, ancient trees, boulders, and so on who had the ability to hold simple conversations in the common tongue. But...they are all gone now. Most were vanquished by the Integrity Knights, while others were harvested by Administrator for their object resources."

"I see...like the guardian dragon whose bones sleep in the cave beneath the northern mountains..."

"Indeed. I took pity on them and, whenever possible, took newly generated AIs under my wing. The familiars I use as my agents are mostly miniature units without a thought engine, but some are the AIs that I put to my own uses, like Charlotte. Because they are so statistically powerful, there is little fear of them being damaged, even when shrunken down. That is how she was safe hiding in your clothes, even with all of your wild thrashing in combat."

"B-but...but...," I stammered, staring at the tiny body in Cardinal's palm as I fought back tears, "Charlotte's speech and behavior wasn't that of a mimic AI. She saved me. She sacrificed herself for me. Why...? How could she...?"

"As I'm sure I told you before, she's been alive for over fifty years. She spent all that time in contact with me and watching over many people. It's already been two years since I put her on you...One doesn't need a fluctlight to develop an attachment over that much time together..."

Cardinal's voice got firmer, more insistent. "Even if the nature of that intelligence is nothing more than an accumulation of input and output data, a true heart can reside within it. Even love, at times. But I don't suppose *you* would ever understand, Administrator—you empty husk!!"

The little wise woman glared up at her two-hundred-year foe, her voice righteous and bold. But the pontifex, still watching the situation unfold from her floating position across the room, did not respond. She merely steepled her fingers in front of her mouth, mirror eyes shining enigmatically.

According to what Cardinal had said in the library, when Administrator fused with the original form of the Cardinal System, the self-correcting process—which was the basis for her second personality, the one that was in Cardinal's form now—was powerful enough that she had to manipulate her own fluctlight to remove her emotions in order to counteract Cardinal's rebellion.

Once the two split into separate bodies, she no longer had to worry about the subprocess taking over her body, but her emotions were still meaningless noise to her and unnecessary to bring back.

So the image of Administrator that I'd carried in my head was that of a programmed human, someone who mechanically carried out her tasks. But the pontifex I saw at the top of Central Cathedral was far from what I'd expected. She sneered at Chudelkin and toyed cruelly with our lives; something told me the grin that she constantly wore was no false simulation.

Even now, the silver-haired, silver-eyed young woman burbled and giggled behind her hands, her eyes narrowing with pleasure. "Heh-heh-heh."

She laughed, slender shoulders rocking, letting Cardinal know that her righteous missive was no more damaging to her than a slight breeze. Eventually, between her chuckles came a short message that made real the very thing I'd been afraid of.

"I thought you'd show up. Heh. Heh-heh-heh."

"I figured that if I picked on these children enough, you'd poke your head out of that musty little burrow of yours. That's the limit of what you can do, little one. You can arrange for pawns who will come after me, but you can't bring yourself to abuse them like the pawns they are. You humans are such helpless creatures."

I knew it...

As I feared, Administrator's true intention was to put enough pressure on us to lure Cardinal out from her isolated library. Or in other words, she did this knowing that she still had a secret trick that would absolutely ensure her triumph.

But the Sword Golem, which ought to have been her ultimate weapon, was virtually destroyed, and now Eugeo and I were perhaps battle capable again. Even Alice was awake, pushing herself up with one hand in an attempt to get up.

Cardinal and Administrator were two sides of the same coin, and in a one-on-one fight would surely draw, so in these circumstances, our presence gave our side an overwhelming advantage, I assumed.

That meant that the instant the door to the library had opened, Administrator's rational choice would have been to stop observing and simply attack at full power without delay. So why had she let Cardinal destroy the Sword Golem and heal Alice and me and even allowed us to have a brief conversation?

Cardinal had to be wondering the same thing—but her expression betrayed nothing but firm determination. "Hmph. In the myriad years since I saw you last, you've learned to affect a passable human being. Been practicing smiling into a mirror for two hundred years, have you?" she mocked.

Administrator shrugged off the comment with that very smile. "And that way of speaking, tiny one. So wise and scholarly! When I had you dragged before me two hundred years ago, you were trembling and alone...Weren't you, Lyserith?"

"Do not call me by that name, Quinella! My name is Cardinal, and I am the program that exists solely to eliminate *you*!"

"Hee-hee, yes, of course. And I am Administrator, the one who manages all programs. So rude of me to have waited so long to introduce myself, my little one. It just took a while for me to prepare the formula in order to welcome you." She gleefully raised her right hand.

Her outstretched fingers curled, as if they were grabbing and crushing some invisible object. At this point, her pure-white cheeks, which had seemed impervious to any rise in emotion, actually flushed with the faintest trace of red blood, and a ghastly look came into her mirror eyes. A chill raced up my back as I realized this was the very first time I had seen her utilizing her full focus and concentration.

But there was no time to act. In an instant, Administrator's right hand clenched fully shut.

Craaaash!! Dozens of heavy shattering sounds burst from every direction in a deafening chorus. My first thought was that the giant glass walls that surrounded the room had all exploded at once.

But that wasn't the case.

What had shattered was *beyond* the windows—the dark, roiling clouds, the blanket of stars, the cold full moon, and the very night sky itself.

The sky rained into an impossible number of fragments, which collided and burst into even smaller pieces as they fell. To my dumbfounded eyes, what appeared after the pieces of literal sky fell could only be described as "unbeing."

A void of black and purple that seemed to have no depth, swirling and marbled, churning away. It was a world of nothing, the kind of sight that would suck away the mind of whoever stared at it for long enough.

In terms of color and beauty they were nothing alike, but I couldn't help but be reminded of another scene I'd witnessed—when the original Aincrad had collapsed, and a veil of white had appeared to swallow the sunset that remained behind.

Had the Underworld just collapsed and vanished as well? The human realm, the Dark Territory, the villages and towns…and all the people living within them…

The only thing that saved me from this momentary terror was Cardinal's shocked but still resolute voice.

"You…you cut the address loose."

What does that mean…?

Despite my confusion, I couldn't tear my eyes away from Administrator. The silver-haired woman lowered her hand and said in a whisper, "Two hundred years ago, I made the mistake of letting you get away when I absolutely had the chance to kill you. That was *me* who placed your stinking little hole on a nonconsecutive address, wasn't it? So I decided to learn from my mistake. I knew that if I could lure you out, I'd trap you on *this* side—the rat in the cage with the cat who hunts her."

The pontifex snapped her fingers to punctuate this statement. Instantly, there was another crashing noise, but much quieter than the last, and the dark-brown door that stood on its own in the middle of the carpet shattered. The pieces split apart before they hit the ground and vanished. Even the circle on the ground that was meant to indicate the location of the elevator platform was gone.

Eugeo was standing right next to it, and he reached out his foot to step on the carpet several times with surprise. Then he looked up, straight at me, and shook his head quickly.

In other words, what Administrator had destroyed wasn't the outside world itself but the connection between this floor of the cathedral and the outside.

Even if we could somehow destroy the windows, there would be no way out of them—there was no *space* there to travel through. It was the perfect way to trap someone in a virtual space—almost *too* perfect—and the exact kind of thing that only someone with admin privileges could do. The prison area in Blackiron Palace on the first floor of Aincrad was child's play compared to this.

In short, Administrator hadn't been wasting her time in the minutes since Cardinal had appeared. She'd been preparing this exact tremendous command for execution.

However, if the consecutive connection between spaces had been completely severed, then...

"I find your analogy lacking in precision," shot back Cardinal, who'd arrived at my conclusion a second before I did. "It might take minutes to sever the connection, but patching it back together will not be so easy. Now you are trapped in here as well. So which of us is really the cat, and which is the rat? We have four in number, and you are alone. If you think these youngsters are beneath your notice, your mistake is grave indeed, Quinella."

She was exactly right.

This now meant that Administrator couldn't easily leave this place, either. And she and Cardinal had identical power when it came to using sacred arts. While her and Cardinal's arts were at a perfect equilibrium, the rest of us could cut her to ribbons and seize victory.

But Cardinal's correction did not wipe the little smile off the pontifex's face.

"Four against one? No...your numbers are off. It's actually four against three hundred. And that doesn't even include me," she gloated.

Just then, the upturned mass of metal—the almost totally destroyed Sword Golem—let out a discordant, eardrum-rending screech.

"What...?!" shouted Cardinal. She'd hit it with three devastating lightning bolts in a row and clearly assumed it was out of commission. I had certainly thought so, at least.

But the golem's eyes, which had been completely dark just seconds ago, were now glittering like twin stars. It fixed us with a murderous glare, pushed itself up with its arms, and got to its four feet as though all the damage it had suffered was instantly gone. When it stood, it let out a belly-wrenching roar.

That was when I noticed that the various sword parts that had been charred and smoking from Cardinal's lightning bolts were gleaming like brand-new weapons.

It was true that weapons with a high-priority value had natural life-restoring capabilities in this realm, but only if they were cared for and put back into their sheaths. Even then, it supposedly took an entire day to recover half of an object's total life, and beyond any of that, the swords that made up the golem's body had been just decorative objects stuck to the room's support pillars—they didn't *have* sheaths.

Even if every part of the golem was a Divine Object type of weapon, they still could not recover so much damage so quickly. But the giant made of swords standing behind the pontifex looked just like it had before the lightning hit it—even more powerful than before, actually. It occurred to me that if she could mass-produce these golems, she might actually rebuff a full-scale invasion from the Dark Territory after all.

I stood there in mute shock until I heard the little sage command, "Kirito, Alice, Eugeo, get behind me! Do not allow yourselves to slip forward!"

I was already behind her, so the other two rushed over. Alice seemed completely healed after being impaled through the chest, in fact. She'd lost her golden breastplate, and the blue knight's corsage beneath was torn, but I didn't get the sense that her flesh was injured under it.

She bravely squared her shoulders and held up the Osmanthus Blade, whispering, "Kirito...who is this person...?"

"...Her name's Cardinal. She fought with Administrator two hundred years ago and was banished. She's another pontifex, basically."

And if one was Administrator, the other was Formatter—the one who would mercilessly reset the world to nothing.

But I couldn't explain all that now, of course. Alice still seemed

suspicious, so I added, "It's all right—she's on our side. She rescued me and Eugeo and showed us the way to get here. She loves this world with all her heart and mourns what it has become."

That, at least, was all true. Alice wasn't over her confusion and doubt yet, but she pressed her hand to her right breast, to the spot where Cardinal's miraculous power had healed her, and nodded deeply.

"...I understand. High-level sacred arts reflect the heart of the caster...and after the way she healed my wounds, I trust in the warmth of her strength."

I nodded back at her. She was absolutely right. Whether the sacred arts caster was hastily tossing off a healing effect or truly putting their prayer into it made a big difference in the effect of the healing art, even when it came to the simplest and quickest of commands.

Cardinal's healing arts were full of true compassionate love. They engulfed and melted away all pain. That was why I hoped there was still room to talk her out of her plan to reinitialize the Underworld—but only if we actually won this battle.

First, we had to figure out the secret of how the Sword Golem had instantly healed itself of all damage, and how we could counteract that.

It began moving forward, its dark-gold body gleaming in the light. Cardinal readied her staff at once, but she couldn't get the jump on it with a major attack in advance like she had a few minutes ago. Administrator would be waiting with eagle eyes to strike at the moment Cardinal started chanting her commands.

Think, think, think. It's all I can do right now.

Most likely, the Sword Golem's auto-healing ability had something to do with Memory Release. So whatever object was the source of the thirty swords that made up the golem's body, it had properties that enabled that effect.

The first thing that popped into my head when I imagined natural healing of life was the Gigas Cedar, the source of the sword in my hand now. But that healing power was fueled by the spatial resources it sucked in from the sun and the earth.

The only resource in this place was the moonlight coming through the windows from the south. And it couldn't possibly have accumulated enough of that to heal the entirety of its massive body in a single moment. So the source of the Sword Golem was not some natural feature like the Gigas Cedar.

That left only some kind of living object with a healing ability that did not require spatial resources. But Cardinal claimed that all the giant Named Monsters that had once existed in this world were now extinct. And ordinary animal units like bears and cattle didn't have the system priority to achieve power like that. Even tens of thousands of them converted into a single sword would fall far short of the Integrity Knights' Divine Object weapons—that was how little life beasts had naturally. Priority and durability were proportional, so how many hundreds, if not thousands, of massive animal units would you need to create thirty of those weapons...?

Wait.

Hadn't Administrator just said something strange a moment ago?

Four versus *three hundred*.

She hadn't used moving objects like animals to create that Sword Golem. She'd used human units—the people who inhabited this world. Three hundred of them. Enough that their loss would completely eliminate an entire village.

This thought process happened in a span so short, my brain cells were practically frying—and I innately sensed that my hunch was true. But there was no triumph in this realization. The only thing I felt was overwhelming terror. My skin was crawling, from my toes up to my spine and the back of my neck.

Underworldians weren't just mobile objects. They had fluctlights—human souls—just like any person in the real world. And their fluctlights would be active as long as they had bodies, even if they'd been converted into something like a sword.

Perhaps the people who'd been turned into those golem parts were still conscious, trapped inside metal without eyes or ears or mouths to speak.

Cardinal reached the same conclusion as I did. Her small body tensed imperceptibly. The hand that clutched her staff was white with the pressure.

"…You wretch." Her youthful voice cracked with rage, betraying the weight of her full age. "Wretched thing…Is there no depth to which you will not sink?! You are their ruler! Your duty is to *protect* the subjects you turned into those swords!!"

"Subjects…? Like…human…beings?" gasped Eugeo, falling back a step.

"You mean…that monster is…human?" moaned Alice, putting her hand to her chest.

Cold, tense silence filled the room. Administrator drank in our shock, fear, and anger. With a gloating smile, she said, "Very good. You finally figured it out, did you? I was getting worried that you'd all be wiped out before I could reveal the big secret."

The supreme ruler laughed, a true laugh of pure delight, and clapped her hands together. "But," she continued, "I'm disappointed in you, little one. After two hundred years of hiding in your den, you still don't fully understand me. In a sense, I am your mother, after all."

"…Enough japes! I'm fully aware of just how depraved your madness is!"

"Then why would you say these silly things? About duties and subjects to be protected. Of *course* I would never bother with such trifling matters."

Her happy smile did not change, but I could sense the atmosphere around Administrator growing rapidly chilly. It was like her lips were absolute zero and the words that came from them were particles of ice in the air. "I am a conqueror. As long as what I rule remains in the lower world in the state that I desire to rule it in—whether human or sword—then there is no real problem."

"You...evil..." Cardinal's voice creaked and cracked. I couldn't think of anything to say, either.

Whatever form the mind of the woman—the *being*—known as Administrator took now was beyond my understanding. She was literally a systems manager and viewed the people of her world as nothing more than data files that could be manipulated and rewritten as she saw fit. Like some Internet addict who downloaded massive numbers of files for the sole purpose of collecting and organizing, without much fussing over what they actually contained.

In our conversation at the Great Library, Cardinal told me that the fundamental purpose burned into Administrator's soul was "maintaining the world." She was probably correct about that, but I felt it didn't fully capture the truth of the situation.

The original Cardinal System in the old *Sword Art Online* was a soulless management program. Did it actually recognize its players as human beings...as living things with individual wills of their own?

The answer to that was no.

We were nothing but data meant to be managed, selected, and deleted.

Maybe Quinella, the little girl who'd existed centuries ago, couldn't kill a person.

But to Administrator, even human beings were no more than fodder.

"Oh, you've all gone quiet. What's the matter?" she said, tilting her head curiously as she surveyed us from on high. "You aren't alarmed by a little thing like matter conversion for a measly three hundred units, are you?"

"Measly...?" Cardinal repeated, her voice barely audible.

"Yes, little one. 'Measly,' 'just,' 'no more than.' How many fluctlights do you think collapsed before I completed this puppet? And this is only the prototype. In order to mass-produce the finished version that can counteract that nasty stress test, I expect I'll need about half."

"Half...of...?"

"Half. Half is half. Half of all the human units that exist in the world...so about forty thousand units. I think that ought to be enough to put a stop to the Dark Territory's invasion and take the fight back to them," she said, a horror show without a hint of irony or doubt.

Then she turned her silver eyes on the knight standing to my left. "Are you satisfied, Alice?" she giggled. "Your precious realm will be quite safe, you see now."

Alice said nothing. I noticed that the hand holding the hilt of her Osmanthus Blade was trembling, but I couldn't tell whether it was from fear or rage.

Ultimately, her answer came in the form of a question, her voice compressed so that nothing showed in it. "Pontifex...it is clear that no words can reach you now. So I ask you as a fellow user of sacred arts. Where are the owners of the thirty swords that make up that giant puppet?"

I was momentarily confused. It was Administrator who had used Memory Release on the thirty swords, transforming them into the golem. So while it broke from the traditional pattern, it would stand to reason that she was their owner. But what Alice said next shattered that assumption.

"It is not possible for you to be the owner. Even if you were to break the basic rule that one can only achieve Perfect Control over one sword, there is no breaking the next one. To perform Memory Release, there *must* be a powerful bond between the sword and its owner. Like me and the Osmanthus Blade, the other knights and their divine weapons, even Kirito and Eugeo and their swords. The master must love the sword and be loved by it. If the source of the swords that make up that puppet are innocent people, then there is no way they would love you for what you did to them!!" Alice declared, her voice ringing loud and clear.

"Heh-heh-heh-heh," Administrator chuckled, breaking the silence that followed. "What is it with you young, foolish souls that makes you so vivacious? This sentimental quality, as sour as a fresh-picked apple...Why, I could just crush you in my fist and slurp down every last drop of juice right now."

Her mirror eyes sparkled with a continuum of color, perhaps reflecting her rising excitement. "But not yet. It is not yet the time, no. What I believe you're trying to say, Alice, is that I cannot make use of enough imagination to overwrite all of these swords. You are correct about this. I do not have enough capacity in my memory to record highly detailed records of every one of these weapons."

She pointed regally toward the thirty swords that made up the Sword Golem, which was still inching onward.

From what I understood, Perfect Weapon Control involved taking one's memory of all the information about a weapon—its appearance, feeling, weight, and so on—and, with the help of spoken commands, altering the weapon itself using the power of the imagination.

In other words, to utilize that ability, the owner of the sword absolutely needed all the information about the weapon to be stored in their head.

For example, if I were to use Perfect Weapon Control with my black sword, I would first need Information A about the sword as it existed in the Main Visualizer of the Lightcube Cluster to match Information B about the sword as it existed in my own fluctlight, with an absolute minimum of discrepancy. By doing so, I could then use my imagination to change Information B and thus overwrite Information A in the process, which would then share that change in information with everyone else. This logic also applied to the strange visual transformation that had come over me earlier.

As for Administrator, her lightcube memory was compacted to its limit by the memories of three hundred years of life. She couldn't possibly keep a picture-perfect memory of all thirty of those swords. Alice's convictions were clearly based on emotion and belief, but unbeknownst to her, it was accurate in terms of the underlying system's limitation as well.

So that meant that each of the swords that made up the golem would have to have its own separate owner. Souls that held those swords in their memories and that had the wicked will to use them for destruction.

But where? In every sense of the word, this space was currently isolated from the outside world. It didn't make sense unless those owners were inside the chamber with us...

"The answer is right before your eyes," she said, suddenly looking right at me. Then her eyes shifted sideways. "Eugeo should understand by now."

"...?!"

I looked over at Eugeo on the other side of Alice, not daring to breathe.

My flaxen-haired partner was staring the pontifex directly in the eyes, not budging, his face completely bloodless and pale. His brown eyes were almost oddly devoid of expression, in fact. Then he craned his neck, trembling, to look up at the ceiling.

I followed his gaze. The rounded ceiling featured a mural that depicted the creation of the world, embedded with little crystals that glittered in the light.

Up until now, I'd assumed this was all decorative. But in Eugeo's blank expression, his eyes were the only thing that emoted, staring holes into the ceiling, searching fiercely for something.

At last, words came croaking from his throat. "Oh...of course."

"What did you figure out, Eugeo?!" I asked. He glanced over at me, his face full of profound fear.

"Kirito...those crystals stuck into the ceiling. Those aren't just...decorations. I think they must be the memory fragments... that were stolen from the Integrity Knights."

"Wha...?" I gaped. So did Cardinal and Alice.

The Integrity Knights' memories.

The most important of memories, the things extracted from

the subjects through the Synthesis Ritual so they could be turned into knights. In most cases, this would, rather obviously, be the memories of their most beloved person. For Eldrie, it was his mother. For Deusolbert, his wife.

So did this mean those crystals were the owners of the swords that made up the Sword Golem?

No. The crystals were just isolated information that was stored in the fluctlight. They weren't entire souls with the independent ability to think. It just couldn't be possible for them to link with the swords and activate Perfect Control.

But then...something prickled in the back of my head.

If all those crystals were the memory fragments taken from Integrity Knights, then that must include the memories of Alice when she was synthesized six years ago.

This was the top floor of Central Cathedral.

When we fought the band of goblins in the cave north of Rulid two years ago, Eugeo was gravely injured. While healing him, I heard a very strange voice speaking.

It sounded like a young girl who claimed that she was waiting for Eugeo and me on the top floor of the cathedral. Then a huge rush of spiritual power flowed through me and healed Eugeo.

What if that voice was coming from Alice's memory fragment? Did that mean the stolen memory itself had some power of independent thought?

But still, all sacred arts operated on that principle of direct contact. Even Administrator herself couldn't send her voice and healing power from Central Cathedral all the way to Rulid, nearly five hundred miles away.

The only way a miracle like that could happen was if the same overwriting logic that Perfect Weapon Control worked on could also apply here. Which would mean the memories stored in Alice's memory crystal were...were...

Cardinal's furious shout cut off my train of thought. "I see...So that's what this is! Oh, Quinella...you have gone too far...This is depraved manipulation of the highest order!!"

Jarred loose from my thoughts, I focused once again on the serene smile of the silver-haired overlord.

"Well, well...I suppose I should give you my compliments, little one. You figured it out faster than I expected for a bleeding-heart altruist. So tell me: What is your answer?"

"It's the fluctlight's shared pattern. It is, isn't it?!" Cardinal said, leveling her black staff at Administrator. "By placing the memory piece you extract during the Synthesis Ritual into a mental model loaded into a fresh lightcube, you can treat it like a simulated human unit. But its intelligence is severely limited that way—essentially no more than a series of instinctive impulses—and it is far from able to execute complex commands like Perfect Weapon Control."

I tried my hardest to process her terminology. Back in the library, Cardinal had said that babies in this world started as fluctlight prototypes loaded on new lightcubes and given a portion of their parents' physical traits and mental and behavioral patterns. So this had to be a similar idea. But instead of starting with information from parents, these came from memory fragments taken from the knights.

In other words, the crystals shining in the ceiling were babies raised on memories of some beloved person. But if that was the case, how could that "Alice" have talked to me two years ago? No newborn child could speak as convincingly as that. The questions kept piling up in my mind.

Cardinal continued, "But there is a shortcut past that limitation. The fact that the memory piece placed in the fluctlight prototype and the structural information of the linked weapon share almost entirely identical patterns. Meaning..."

She paused to smack the butt of her staff hard against the ground and shouted, "That you created those swords using the very beloved that you stole from the Integrity Knights' memories. Didn't you, Administrator?!"

Once the initial confusion of this accusation died down, I was assaulted by such overwhelming fear and disgust that I felt my entire body turn to ice.

The owners of the swords that made up the golem were the fluctlights that had been made from the Integrity Knights' stolen memories.

The swords themselves were crafted using the people in those memories—Eldrie's mother, Deusolbert's wife, and probably other close family members—as a base material. That was Cardinal's accusation.

Once they belatedly understood the implications, Eugeo and Alice uttered simultaneous grunts of shock and horror.

If it was true, then perhaps it was theoretically possible to execute Memory Release. After all, Information A in the Main Visualizer and Information B in the fluctlight were coming from the exact same individual. If the newborn fluctlight with the memory fragment in it felt something strongly enough about the sword it was linked to, it was possible.

The problem was what that "something" would be. The memory fragments shouldn't have had more advanced minds than a newborn baby. What impulse, what emotion could they be feeling that would control that mammoth Sword Golem...?

"Desire," said Administrator, practically reading my thoughts. "Desire to touch. To squeeze. To make one's own. Those are the ugly urges that drive this sword creation."

"Heh-heh. Heh-heh-heh." She narrowed her eyes. "The simulated personas made from the knights' memory fragments all desire just one thing: to own the one person they remember, whoever it is. They're stuck up there in the ceiling, but they can sense that person is right nearby. They just can't touch them. They can't be one. Afflicted by maddening hunger and thirst, all they see are enemies that keep them from what they want and need. If they just kill those enemies, then whoever they want will finally be theirs. So they fight. No matter how much they suffer or how often they fall, they'll get back up and fight for eternity.

What do you think...? It's lovely, isn't it? The things the power of desire can achieve...they are tremendous!"

Her voice rang out on high. The approaching Sword Golem's eyes flickered violently. A harmonic roar—which now sounded to me like a scream of grief and despair—erupted from its vicious form.

It wasn't just an automated weapon designed to slaughter. It was a poor, pathetic lost child, driven by nothing more than the hope to see that one person it knew again.

Administrator said desire was the power that moved the golem. But...

"—You're wrong!!" shouted Cardinal, just as the thought entered my head. "Do not disgrace the emotion of wanting to see someone again, to touch them again, with a word like *desire*! This is...this is pure love!! The greatest power and final miracle of humanity...and it is not to be weaponized by the likes of you!!"

"They are the same thing, little one," said Administrator, her lips twisted with happiness. She extended her palms toward the Sword Golem. "Love is control...Love is desire! It is nothing more than a signal that is output from the fluctlight! All I did was take that signal, the most firm and powerful of any you can get, and use it effectively. I did it much, much better than your way!!"

Her voice rose to a fever pitch, as if she was certain of her triumph. "The best that you could achieve was ensnaring two or three powerless children. But I am different. The puppet I created runs on the overflowing energy of over three hundred units' desire, including the memory fragments! And most important of all..."

She paused for dramatic effect, preparing the final poison stinger.

"...Now that you know the truth, you *cannot* destroy it. Because now you know that my puppet is actually living human beings turned into swords!!" she announced, her words trailing off in the long silence.

Stunned, I watched as Cardinal's staff slowly dropped from

its position pointed at the Sword Golem. When she spoke, it was almost bizarrely calm.

"Yes...that is right. I cannot commit murder. That is a limitation I can never break...I spent two hundred years devising an art that would kill you and your inhuman form...but it would seem my efforts are for naught."

I was stunned. She'd admitted her defeat just as simply as that.

But if the weapons in the Sword Golem were indeed living people, then Cardinal could not end those lives...She would not even attempt it. Even if, like with the teacups and soup cups, there was some way around that limitation.

"Heh-heh. Heh-heh-heh-heh."

Administrator's lips curled up as far as they could go, her throat convulsing with unstoppable laughter amid the shocked silence. "How foolish you were...What a tragic comedy..."

"Ha-ha-ha-ha."

"You should've known. You know the true nature of this world. You know that the 'life' around us is just a collection of data that can be changed and rewritten. Yet you treat that data as human, binding yourself to the rule against murder...Truly, there can be no greater folly..."

"They *are* human, Quinella," Cardinal remonstrated. "The people who live in the Underworld have the true emotions that we lost. They laugh, grieve, rejoice, and love. What more does one need to be human? Whether the container of that soul is a lightcube or a biological brain is of little matter. This I believe. And thus—I accept my defeat with pride."

The mention of the word *defeat* gouged deep into my chest. But that was nothing compared to what she said next.

"But I have one condition. I will give you my life...but in exchange, I ask you not to take the lives of these young ones."

"...!!"

I held my breath and started to step forward, while Eugeo and Alice froze with shock. But the sheer willpower radiating from Cardinal's figure stopped me short.

Administrator narrowed her eyes like a cat with her prey in her claws and wondered, "Oh…but what do I stand to gain by accepting this condition of yours?"

"As I said, I've been preparing an art for you. If you seek battle, I could keep your pitiable puppet at bay *and* tear away half of your remaining life. With that much stress, your uncertain memory capacity might be in even worse peril, no?"

"Mmmm…," she murmured, putting a finger to her cheek and pretending to think without breaking her smile. "Well, I don't feel that my fluctlight is threatened by a battle whose outcome is already known. But I suppose it would be a bother…and when you say to spare 'the lives of the young ones,' would sending them back to the lower world from this isolated space fulfill that condition? If you say I can never do anything to harm them for all eternity, I refuse."

"No, just a momentary evacuation is all I ask. I trust in them to…"

Cardinal did not finish that sentence. Instead, she turned on her heel, robe swaying, and looked at me with kindness in her eyes.

I wanted to scream that this was ridiculous. My temporary life here and Cardinal's one and only life were not equal. If anything, I was seriously considering throwing myself at Administrator to buy *Cardinal* time to escape instead.

But I couldn't do that. I couldn't risk Eugeo's and Alice's lives on my own suicidal gamble. I clutched my sword so hard my hand hurt and my foot creaked with the pressure against the floor. I was caught between impulse and reason.

"Hmph. Fine," said Administrator, her beautiful mouth forming a smirk. "That gives me another game to look forward to later. Right? So you have my word to Stacia. I will take the little one—"

"No, don't swear to any god. Swear to the one thing that you actually think has absolute value: your own fluctlight," Cardinal interrupted.

A slightly exasperated note entered Administrator's smile,

but she nodded again. "Fine, fine, I'll swear to the precious data accumulated in my fluctlight. And once I've killed you, I'll let the other three go unharmed. That pledge is the one thing I cannot break…for now."

"Good," said Cardinal. She gave a look to both Eugeo and Alice and lastly, turned to me. There was a gentle smile on her young face, and nothing but benevolent kindness in her brown eyes. I couldn't stop the emotions in my chest from spilling out as liquid and blotting my vision.

Her lips opened and silently mouthed the words *I'm sorry.*

In the distance, Administrator called out a triumphant goodbye to her victim. She waved her hand, and the Sword Golem stopped where it was, near the center of the room.

Then she made a clenching gesture, hand still held high, and glittering bits of light came dancing out of empty air, coalescing into a long, slender shape.

The object that emerged was a silver rapier. It was as thin as a needle, with a beautifully curved guard, all of it perfectly silver in color. It was so delicate that it almost seemed decorative, but the overwhelming aura surrounding it spoke to its priority value and made it hard to breathe even at a distance.

Like Cardinal's black staff, this was Administrator's personal weapon—the ultimate source of the power that supported her sacred arts.

The silver rapier rang like a bell when she pointed it straight at Cardinal. The sage faced her directly, showing no fear of the divine weapon trained upon her heart, and walked forward.

Alice and Eugeo leaned forward, as though they were going to chase after her. But I held my hand out to keep them back. Deep down, I wanted to swing my sword right through Administrator, of course. But giving in to my emotions now would only waste Cardinal's determination and sacrifice. I had to hold back my tears, grit my teeth, and stay put.

Rainbows of sheer delight cascaded through Administrator's

eyes as she stared down at her counterpart. Then a bolt of lightning shot from the tip of the rapier, painting the entire chamber
white for a split second as it pierced Cardinal's little body.

In the center of the blurred wall of white that was my vision,
I saw a silhouette bend backward as though it had been flicked.

The energy of the beyond-massive lightning bolt charred the
air as it dispersed, and I struggled to keep my eyes open as it
threatened to bowl me over.

The youthful sage hadn't actually fallen yet. She leaned on
her long staff, feet planted firmly into the carpet, face resolutely
pointed at her archenemy.

But the signs of damage were ghastly. Her black hat and robe
were ragged and smoking, and part of her proud, shining curls
was burned so badly it was basically ash.

As we watched in silent horror just fifteen feet away, Cardinal
lifted her left hand and brushed off her charred hair. When she
spoke, her voice was ragged but loud. "Hmph...So this is all...
y-you're capable of. Fire as many as you want...but you can't—"

Krakowww!!

Another mammoth thunderbolt shook the world.

A lightning bolt even greater than the first one rocketed out
of Administrator's rapier, mercilessly tearing through Cardinal.
Her pointed hat flew off and evaporated into tiny shards. Her
body twitched in agony, slumped to the side, and escaped falling
over entirely only by going to one knee.

"Oh, but of course I'm going easy on you, my little one,"
Administrator whispered, just barely holding back her mad exultation. "It would be too boring if I finished you off all at once. I've
been waiting two hundred years for this...*moment!!*"

Craaak!! A third blast.

This one arced overhead and struck Cardinal like a whip, slamming her against the ground with terrifying force. She bounced
high and collapsed to the ground again, where she lay limply.

Half of her velvet robe was charred cinders now, and there were more burnt holes in the white blouse and black knickers underneath it. Her skin was white as snow before, but now there were burn marks like black snakes running along her limbs.

Still, her arm pressed into the carpet, trying to lift her body off it. As if just to mock this tiny act—practically the last ounce of strength Cardinal could have had left—Administrator hit her with another lightning bolt sideways. The little girl was blasted into the air and rolled several yards away across the floor.

"Heh…heh-heh. Heh-heh-heh." From her distant height, Administrator's laughter spilled forth, as though she couldn't hold it back any longer. "Heh-heh, ah-ha. Ah-ha-ha-ha-ha."

Her mirror eyes had neither white nor iris. Instead, brilliant refracted rainbow light swirled through them. "Ah-ha-ha-ha-ha! Ha-ha-ha-ha-ha-ha!!"

She held up the rapier, and from its tip poured a succession of lightning, one bolt after another, endlessly ravaging Cardinal's helpless body. Each one kicked her like a ball, burning away her clothes, her skin, her hair, her very existence.

"Ha-ha-ha-ha-ha!! Ah-ha-ha-ha-ha-ha-ha-ha!!" bellowed Administrator, hair spraying as she writhed in demonic pleasure.

I barely even heard the sound. Tears flooded from my eyes and blurred my vision, and it wasn't because the rampant flashing of lightning was burning them. It was just the only outlet for the storm of feelings that was roaring through me: lamentation that Cardinal's life was slipping away before my eyes, fury at Administrator's delight in her callous execution, but most of all, anger at myself for being powerless to do anything but watch.

I couldn't even ready my sword or take a single step forward. Even if the worst should come to pass and Cardinal's sacrifice was utterly wasted and the voices in my head screamed to use that sword to kill Administrator, my body might as well have been turned to stone for all it listened to me.

And I knew why.

If it was my power of Incarnation that caused my Vorpal Strike to extend far beyond its range to pierce Prime Senator Chudelkin, then that very same power was what turned me into helpless stone now.

When I attacked the Sword Golem minutes ago, I didn't put a dent in it—and its counterattack nearly killed me. The feeling of that cold blade severing my torso left me with a powerful mental image of defeat. Terror gripped my limbs, so powerful that it made me all but certain that I couldn't summon that mental image of being Kirito the Black Swordsman again.

I couldn't beat any Integrity Knight now. Not even the students at Swordcraft Academy. And the idea that I might attack the pontifex was simply laughable.

"*...Nngh...hrrk...*"

I felt my throat convulse and heard the miserable sobs that escaped.

Cardinal knew she was defeated, accepted it, and bravely faced her fate. The thought that she was in the act of giving up her life now and I was going to be saved by abandoning her filled me with a festering self-hatred.

Then I noticed Alice, clenching her teeth, and Eugeo, his body curled, shedding silent tears. I couldn't know what they were feeling, but at the very least, it was clear that they, too, were aware of their own powerlessness.

Even if we escaped with our lives now, what could we possibly do with these mental scars on our souls?

All we could do was watch as presumably the last and largest bolt of lightning infused the rapier, which the young woman brandished on high. "Now...let's finish this—our two-hundred-year game of hide-and-seek. Good-bye, Lyserith. Good-bye, my daughter...and my other self."

It was almost sentimental, if not for the fact that it came from lips twisted with sick joy. She lowered the rapier.

The final attack came surging on a million rays of light, striking Cardinal's prone body, burning it, obliterating it.

The sage's body flew high in the air, right leg disintegrating from its charred state below the knee, and landed at my feet. The sound it made was dry and weightless, like there was no longer any mass to her. Pieces of blackened soot scattered off her skin and melted into thin air.

"Heh-heh…ah-ha-ha-ha…ah-ha-ha-ha-ha! *Aaaah-ha-ha-ha-ha-ha!!*"

Administrator spun the sword in her palm, contorting her upper body like she was doing a dance. "I can see it…I can see your life ebbing away, bit by bit!! Oh, what a beautiful sight… each little droplet like the finest gemstone…Now show me the final act. I will give you just enough time to say your good-byes."

I fell to my knees, as though my body had been waiting to obey that order, and reached out to Cardinal. The right side of her face was charred black, and her left eye was closed. But where I touched her cheek, I felt the slightest warmth of life, just before it could vanish.

Before I knew what I was doing, I had lifted her up with both hands and cradled her to my chest. My tears overflowed, dropping onto her badly burned skin.

Her burned eyelashes fluttered and rose. Even at the moment of her death, Cardinal's dark-brown eyes were full of everlasting love and tenderness.

"Don't cry, Kirito."

She didn't say the words aloud. The concept just entered my consciousness as thought.

"It is not the worst end I could have. I never expected…that I would die in the arms of someone…whose heart I felt a true connection with…"

"I'm sorry…I'm so sorry…," I choked out, hardly more audible than she'd been. Cardinal's lips—miraculously unharmed—curled into a faint grin.

"What…do you have…to apologize for? You still have…a duty… to fulfill. You and Eugeo…and Alice…must find a way…this beautiful…fragile…world…"

Her voice suddenly got much more distant, and I thought I felt her body getting lighter. Kneeling nearby, Alice quickly reached out to engulf Cardinal's right hand with both of her own.

"We will…we will." Her voice and cheeks were wet with tears. "You saved these lives for us…and we will use them to fulfill this mission."

Eugeo's hands reached in from the other side. "I swear, too." He was full of powerful intent, so forthright that it made me wonder whether he was really the same shy, gentle boy I'd known all this time. "At last, I have learned the duty I am meant to fulfill."

But I wasn't expecting the words that came next. Neither was Alice, and perhaps not even Cardinal.

"And the time for me to fulfill it is now, in this moment. I will not run. I have…a duty that must be executed."

4

Powerless.

I'm so powerless.

It was the only thought that Eugeo could entertain as Administrator was charring Cardinal's body with her tremendous bolts of lightning.

The Sword Golem, which seemed like some horrific demon from the land of darkness, had started off just as human as Eugeo. The thought itself was a shock, and the realization that the pontifex was capable of envisioning and creating such a thing made him quake with fear. But what wounded Eugeo deepest of all was the despair that he was unable to do anything about it.

The entire reason that Eugeo, Kirito, Alice, Charlotte the spider, and Cardinal had come to the top floor to battle the supreme ruler was because Eugeo had wished he could save his childhood friend Alice Zuberg from the clutches of the Axiom Church. It was Eugeo who had put them in this terrible situation. It should have been him standing at the very front, fighting and taking all the wounds of battle. It should have been him.

And what did I do?

He'd fallen prey to Administrator's seduction, allowed her to steal his memory, and pointed his sword at his best friend, Kirito. And when he'd finally regained his wits, he'd encased Kirito and

Alice in ice and gone back to the top floor to defeat the pontifex, but he couldn't manage it. In the fight against Chudelkin,
the only thing he'd done was distract the enemy with sacred arts.
And then with the Golem, all he'd done was watch as it had sliced
up Charlotte, Kirito, and Alice.

Am I really this powerless?

*Alice's memory fragment is only a dozen or two mels away...
somewhere in the mural on the ceiling. But I failed to get it back
and survived only through Cardinal's sacrifice, and now I'll be
thrown out of the tower. Is that the end of my journey?*

The pontifex would surely send Eugeo, Kirito, and Alice to far
separate locations. He might not even wind up in Norlangarth
Empire. He might never find Kirito again or get back home to
Rulid. He'd live the rest of his life in a strange, foreign land,
trembling in fear of the Axiom Church's retribution and cursing
his own foolishness and lack of ability...

At the very least, he could keep his eyes open, to fully take in
the blinding flash of the lightning that struck Cardinal.

And then he realized at last: Accepting the offer of banishment
to another realm was the worst possible choice he could make.

The pontifex herself had said she would turn half the people in
the world, forty thousand of them, into swords. A veritable army
of horrifying, tragic monsters to fight against the army of the
land of darkness.

It meant that every family, every couple would be torn apart.
Just like Eldrie and his mother. Like Deusolbert and his wife.
Like Alice and the Zubergs.

And then they'd be turned into the most hideous and horrific
weapons imaginable. It couldn't happen. It mustn't happen.

*Stopping that tragedy is my final duty. That's why I'm here right
now. I don't have Kirito's and Alice's skills with the blade or Cardinal's talent for arts...but I know there's something else I can do.
Don't waste your time lamenting your lack of power, Eugeo—find
a way to fight.*

And so Eugeo stood in place, thinking his hardest.

The Blue Rose Sword was half ice, so it might break the barrier that rebuffed all metal, but if he just swung it at Administrator, she would either blaze him with her lightning or send the golem to slice him to pieces. At best, his Memory Release power might stop her in her tracks for a moment or two.

He couldn't destroy the Sword Golem first, because its one weak point, the Piety Module, was safely stored in its chest, far from his attack range. Even assuming he could reach it, he'd have to strike through the tiny one-cen gap between the three swords that made up its spine—while avoiding the attacks of its rib swords. If that was possible, he'd need the pontifex's ability to fly and armor that deflected sharp blades.

If only he could make his body as hard as ice, like the vision of Blue Rose and permanent ice that he'd seen in the Great Library, and become one with his sword. Become so hard that neither lightning nor flame could stop him...nor any blade cut his skin.

Eugeo's eyes flew open.

There was a way he could do it. There must be.

But even if he could achieve it, there was something else he would need. A power like that which operated the Sword Golem. Some miraculous power that would call forth his Memory Release.

Just then, he felt like he heard someone calling his name.

His gaze was drawn upward to the ceiling.

Running around the side of the massive dome was a mural that depicted the creation of the world. The gods that built the sky and earth. The ancient humans who were allowed to live there. The gods choosing a single priestess and giving her the role of guiding humanity in their stead. The birth of the Axiom Church, and the building of the white tower in the middle of Centoria.

It was the same as the history book that Eugeo had practically devoured while he was in the library. But it was probably all fiction. A story that Administrator had cooked up to make it easier for her to rule humanity.

At the edge of this ceiling of lies, there was a fine picture of a small bird. It had a stalk of barley in its beak and was flying away. This was the blue bird, from the children's story, that took the stalk from the strictly regimented fields of the great nobles and flew it out to the rural areas before it died. At this point in time, it seemed that this might be the one story that was actually true.

The crystal embedded in the bird's eye glittered.

It was a glitter that had been familiar to Eugeo all his life. The light that sparkled in the eyes of the little blond girl his age...

And then Eugeo realized his role to play at last.

5

Eugeo...what are you going to do? I wondered, my eyes darting.

The flaxen-haired youth, my unquestionable best friend, Eugeo the swordsman of the Aincrad style, looked back into my eyes for just a moment and smiled. Then he turned to Cardinal and said, "With what strength you have left, turn me—turn my body into a sword. Just like that puppet."

As though it were bringing her mind back to the surface, this statement caused Cardinal's eyes to sharpen again, widening in surprise.

"Eugeo...are you...?"

"If we escape this place...then Administrator will turn half the people of the world into those horrible monsters. We cannot let that happen. If there's any way to prevent that tragedy, any last hope remaining, then it must be in that sacred art..."

His smile had the serenity of understanding and acceptance. He wrapped her left hand in both of his and whispered, "System Call...Remove Core Protection."

I'd never heard that command before.

Eugeo closed his eyes when he was finished. On his forehead appeared a complex series of glowing purple lines, like some kind of electrical circuit board. They stretched downward, across his cheeks and his throat, to his shoulders, his forearms, his fingers.

The little pathways of light pushed a small amount of the way into Cardinal's left hand where he held it, their ends flickering as though waiting for an input.

Remove Core Protection.

Based on the definition of the English in that command, I assumed that Eugeo had just given Cardinal limitless privileges to manipulate his own fluctlight. I didn't know *how* he knew that art, but at the very least, it was a trio of words that spoke to his utter determination and acceptance.

The dying sage's eyes bulged—one fine, one burned—and her lips trembled. Her uncertain thoughts traveled through skin contact.

"Are you sure...Eugeo? I don't know...if you can be turned...back."

Eugeo closed his eyes, his forehead and cheeks covered in glowing lines, and bobbed his head. "It's all right. This is my role...This is the reason I'm here right now. In fact, there's one thing I need to tell you here at the end. Cardinal...Kirito, and Alice. Metal weapons cannot reach Administrator's body. It's why I wasn't able to stick her with the dagger you gave me."

"...!"

Alice and I gasped and held that breath.

But Cardinal didn't seem surprised at all—or maybe she just didn't have the strength to show that much emotion. Her only response was to blink.

Eugeo bobbed his head and prompted, "Please...do it. Before Administrator notices."

"...No, Eugeo. Stop," I demanded, my throat dry and hoarse. "If you don't...make it back...then...then your dream..."

If we actually won this fight and Eugeo didn't get turned back into a human, then the hopes he'd been holding on to for the last eight years—his dream of getting Alice back and taking her home to Rulid—would never come true.

Administrator and Cardinal were the only two people in the world capable of this ultra-advanced ability to convert people's flesh into weapons. One of them was the ultimate enemy, and the other was at death's door. If this gambit actually succeeded, it could very well leave him with no means to return to human form.

I wanted to continue arguing, but Eugeo turned his purple-lit face up to the ceiling and interrupted, "It's okay, Kirito. This is what I was meant to do."

"...!"

My best friend's mind was made up, and there was nothing I could say to him.

And what *could* I say in such a situation?

One single defeat had me shaken to my core. I couldn't swing my sword or even step forward closer to danger.

Instead, I looked pleadingly at Alice. Her blue eyes were full of pain and respect in equal measure. In the next moment, her head hung low. She bowed to the criminal whom she'd struck without hesitation just two days ago at the academy's great hall.

I bit my lip hard enough to draw blood. In my arms, Cardinal struggled to keep her eyes open. *"Very well, Eugeo. Then I dedicate the very last art of my life...to your decision."*

Like a candle before it burned out, her voice regained a valiant bit of strength inside my mind. Purple glimmers lit up the middle of her brown eyes.

The pathways of light that ran from Eugeo's hands to Cardinal's suddenly flashed. That light raced through Eugeo's body, and when it reached the pattern on his forehead, it emerged as a pillar of light that blazed all the way to the ceiling.

"What—?!"

That was Administrator, who was still looking drunk with exultation on the far side of the room. Instantly, her triumphant expression vanished. Fury crossed her silver eyes, and she bellowed, "You half-dead little whelp! What are you doing?!"

She pointed her rapier at me, Eugeo, and Cardinal. White sparks shot from the body of the weapon.

"No, you don't!!" shouted Alice.

The Osmanthus Blade, which had to be near the end of its

remaining life, disintegrated loudly into a golden chain that flew through the air. At the same time, an earsplitting blast from a giant bolt of lightning came toward us.

The tip of the chain brushed the white bolt. The enemy surge was directed down the length of the chain toward Alice.

But by that point, the golden chain was stretching behind her as well, the far end jammed into the floor. Locked into the ground wire and unable to escape back into the air, the massive burst of energy flowed directly into the tower itself, producing a roar and white smoke before it vanished.

Alice leveled her index finger at Administrator and declared, "Your lightning will not affect me!!"

"Why, you little puppet knight…Don't you dare speak back to me!!" the supreme ruler spat, snarling. Just as quickly, her sublime smile returned, and she held the shining rapier on high. "What about *this*, then?!"

A multitude of red dots popped into being around the weapon, well over thirty. If they were all heat elements, then their number was certainly over the element-controlling limit of twenty for a human being.

The Osmanthus Blade's Perfect Control weakness against shifting flames had been made clear in the battle against Chudelkin earlier. But the golden knight did not give way; in fact, she took one loud, bold step forward, boot clacking against the ground. The golden whip, sensing its master's determination, disintegrated into shards and reformed in a grid pattern.

While the two women faced off, the purple light shining from Eugeo only grew brighter and brighter, until he suddenly slumped powerlessly. Instead of falling to the floor, however, he began to float into the air.

He went into a horizontal position, eyes closed, and all his clothes vanished as though they'd evaporated. The beam of light rising from his forehead touched the ceiling. As though answering his call, one of the pictures in the mural began to twinkle—the little bird soaring through the ancient skies, its eye crystal shining.

The roughly thirty crystals embedded in the ceiling, the memory fragments taken from all the Integrity Knights, should have been active in owning the Sword Golem. Only the bird's crystal was different, pulsing with light as it came free from the ceiling and descended through the beam of light.

And that crystal, perhaps—no, almost certainly—was the memory fragment belonging to Alice.

I suspected that when Alice was synthesized, she'd lost the memory of her sister, Selka. But if that were the case, then Selka would've already been abducted and turned into a sword here by the time I first met her in Rulid two years ago.

So if it wasn't Selka...then who were the memories saved in that crystal about?

The hexagonal prism crystal, pointed on both ends, descended silently, offering no answers. The Blue Rose Sword rose from the floor, rotating, and came to a stop with the tip pointed at Eugeo's heart.

Eugeo's muscled body, the translucent blade of the Blue Rose Sword, and the crystal prism formed one straight line.

Meanwhile, the distant Administrator screamed and swung down her rapier.

"Then you can all *burn*!!"

Thirty heat elements floating around the rapier fused, forming a giant fireball that shot forth.

"And I said...no you don't!!" cried Alice, her voice ringing loud and clear. She pointed her right hand at the swirling flame.

The tiny blades forming a cross in midair swarmed together into a giant shield. The knight leaned against it and pushed off the ground, rushing straight toward the coming fireball.

A crash.

A short silence.

The resulting explosion was big enough to rattle the entirety of the enclosed space. Fire whipped, light flashed, shock waves burst across the chamber, and most of the carpet on the floor burned into nothing. Even the massive Sword Golem, inactive across the room, buckled with the force, and Administrator herself shielded her face with her arm.

But safe behind Alice's shield, the worst I felt was a wave of heat that caused me to gasp. Neither Eugeo floating in the air nor Cardinal in my arms seemed to have been affected by the blast.

Within a few seconds, the maelstrom of flame was gone, as quickly as it'd come...and at its center, Alice fell to the ground with a thud. A second later the Osmanthus Blade, back to its original form, slumped next to its master, point stuck in the ground.

Alice's white-and-blue knight's uniform was charred and smoking here and there. Large burn scars ran over her arms and legs; it was clear from a glance that she was catastrophically wounded. She didn't get up—possibly unconscious—but in the valuable few seconds she bought us, Cardinal managed to finish her command.

Within the pillar of purple light, Eugeo's body lost its solidity and turned invisible. The Blue Rose Sword, also becoming transparent, moved into the center of his chest, fusing with him.

There was another flash.

I squinted against the brightness, and Eugeo unraveled into a million ribbons of light.

Fiercely swirling, they condensed back into a new shape.

What was left floating there was not human in appearance.

It was one mammoth sword, stark white with the faintest hint of blue, and a cross-shaped guard. The blade was as long and wide as Eugeo's actual body. Its slight curve was beautiful, ending in a fiercely sharp point. A little furrow in the raised ridge on the flat of the blade was perfectly sized for the floating crystal to fit inside, and it did, with a little click.

Cardinal's arm fell limply to the floor. Her lips quivered, and the final part of the command escaped like the slightest of breezes.

"Release...Recollection."

Keeeeennn! The double-edged, six-sided crystal, Alice's memory fragment, shone and reverberated. Eugeo's sword rang on its own to answer that call and floated even higher.

Now the white greatsword was moving on its own, using the same logic that powered the Sword Golem. A sword forged from a human body, the fragment of memories that owned the sword, and the energy that bound them together: the power of love.

But there was one thing the Sword Golem had that Eugeo's sword didn't: the Piety Module prism that Administrator had placed in the heart of the golem. That was the tool that twisted the love powering the creature, driving it to murder.

"You'll pay for this meddling, Lyserith!!" shouted Administrator, flinching away from the shine of the greatsword as though it was blinding her. "You can mimic my great creation...That one flimsy sword cannot withstand the might of my killing machine! I'll break it in two!!"

She swung her left hand, and the silent Sword Golem's eyes lit up again. It emitted an unpleasant metallic whine and began to shuffle forward at high speed.

Eugeo's sword rotated until the flat was entirely level, with the point trained straight on the five-mel-tall giant. Its white length shone brighter and brighter, casting off motes of light into the air around it.

Then the greatsword flew, ringing like a bell. It soared, a sharpened comet, leaving a long white trail behind it.

"...*Beautiful*...," Cardinal thought audibly from my arms. "*Human...love. And the radiating light...of purpose...So... beautiful...*"

"Yeah...it is," I whispered, feeling more tears coming to my eyes.

"*Kirito...I leave this to you now...Protect this...world...and its...people...*"

With her last bit of strength, Cardinal turned her head to look at me with eyes crystal clear and smiled. Once she saw me nod my understanding, the little girl who was the world's wisest sage closed her eyes, exhaled—and never drew breath again.

As I fought against the sobs, I felt the weight in my arms grow lighter and lighter. In a world blurred by tears, the white sword that bore Cardinal's last wish flew straight and true on wings of light.

The golden giant spread its arms and ribs wide to welcome this oncomer. The blades took position like gleaming jaws, surrounded by an aura of darkness.

In terms of sheer numerical priority, there was no way that a greatsword based on Eugeo and his Blue Rose Sword alone could compete with a golem converted from three hundred human beings. But Eugeo's sword sped up regardless, charging into the waiting fangs of the beast.

Its tip was pointed right at the middle of the golem's spine—which was made up of three swords in alignment—at the purple light spilling from the cracks between the swords.

The Piety Module.

Gold and white collided for the briefest of moments. White and black light tangled, swirled, burst.

The overlapping metal collisions sounded like some beastly roar, and the golem's arms and ribs slid down to an intersecting point. But just before they could close, the white sword plunged deep into the tiny gap in its backbone.

My ears caught the faintest crackling sound. The purple light seeping from the spine burst into nothing.

From the point where the white greatsword struck, the thirty gigantic blades held together with thick darkness began to sparkle and lighten. It almost felt like Eugeo and Alice's love was repairing the sorrow of all those separated lovers.

Greeeee! A discordant scream came from the creature, gradually resolving into clean, clear harmony, a beautiful musical chord that rang long and loud before dispersing.

Then the killing machine, the creature that had nearly pushed us to death, fell apart into its individual swords and burst. Thirty different swords spun out following thirty different arcs, sticking and clattering on various surfaces around the room in a deafening clamor.

One of them stood directly behind me like a gravestone. It was from the left arm of the golem, the one that had sliced into me, but the aura of evil around it was gone now, and it was just smooth, cold metal again.

The glittering crystals on the ceiling that were controlling the golem blinked unsteadily and lost their light until they were still again. I didn't know what had happened to the "minds" inside of them, but at the very least, Administrator's Perfect Control, which had abused their emotions for power, was broken—never to return, I assumed.

The white greatsword that had destroyed the Sword Golem in a single swing was still levitating flat in the air, beams of light shining off it.

Glistening in the center of the blade was Alice's memory fragment. Like a bolt from the heavens, I suddenly understood what was contained within it.

Thirty-one Integrity Knights. But only thirty swords in the Sword Golem. The fusion with Eugeo's sword made it clear that the only memory fragment that hadn't been used for that purpose was Alice's.

So why couldn't Administrator forge a sword that would pair up with Alice's memories?

It must've been because Alice's memories...her love...was too great. Young Alice loved Eugeo, loved Selka, loved her parents, loved everyone who lived in the village, loved Rulid itself, and even loved the time in which the people she loved lived and would continue to live.

Even the almighty pontifex couldn't convert time and space into solid matter. So she wasn't able to make a sword she could link to Alice. And it was why the sword that Alice and Eugeo made was so beautiful and radiant.

"Yes...it really is beautiful," I whispered to Cardinal's soul, which was now traveling to a place much farther than anywhere in the Underworld or the real world, as I clutched her body.

She didn't speak back, but I felt her tiny body taking on a faint phosphorescence in my arms. It was the exact same kind of purity of being that I felt from the white sword's miracle light.

This, to me, was the proof that Cardinal, who was once a girl named Lyserith, was not simply a program, as she claimed so many times, but a true human being with real emotions and love.

The glow brought a gentle warmth that penetrated my freezing flesh, even as her body began to lose its solidity. It was becoming transparent, until at last the contours broke apart, and she vanished in a spray of light.

The waves lit every surface of the isolated-chamber, purifying it all—until they were ripped apart by a voice like a blade that resisted everything.

"That was a very vexing stunt to play right at your death, little one. You've put a very nasty scar on my long-awaited memory of triumph."

Even after the destruction of her ultimate weapon, Administrator was as haughty as she'd ever been, a cold smile on her lips. "But the best she could do was destroy one measly prototype. I can make hundreds of them, thousands."

The way she boasted about this with her rapier in hand was so mechanical, so utterly artificial, that it truly made me wonder, despite her having the same origins as Cardinal, whether she had actually lost her ability to feel emotion. Her shining white skin and dazzling silver hair exuded pulses of darkness like some kind of miasma.

Deep inside me, the cold serpent of fear bared its fangs once again. On instinct, I clutched my now empty arms together.

The seemingly invincible Sword Golem was destroyed, but at a tremendous cost. We'd lost the sage who was the only person in the world capable of counteracting Administrator's overwhelming power.

All I could do was stare up at the pontifex in silent horror—but

Eugeo's sword kept rising, and with a smooth ringing sound, it pointed directly at our last and greatest foe.

"Oh?" Administrator's mirror eyes narrowed. "You still want to fight, little boy? A little bit overconfident, just because you managed to stick in the gap and destroy my puppet, don't you think?"

I couldn't even be sure whether her words were registering with Eugeo while he was in sword form. But the pure-white blade steadfastly held its tip in her direction. The shine that surrounded the weapon grew stronger, its vibrating pitch growing higher and higher.

"...Stop it, Eugeo," I rasped, reaching out toward the shining sword. "Don't...don't go alone."

Driven by a burning panic, I shuffled over the charred carpet on weakened knees. I stretched as far as I could toward the sword and touched one of the motes of light that came off it, but the mote burst and vanished.

Out of the handle of the greatsword, another set of wings made of light grew. The wings flapped hard, pushing the white weapon directly at Administrator.

A wicked grin appeared on her pearly lips. Her mirrored rapier creaked as she swung it down, and another blast of lightning, perhaps even bigger than the ones that killed Cardinal, burst forward to meet the rushing sword of light.

The instant the lightning touched the tip of the sword, there was an even greater shock wave than the one that had started upon the Sword Golem's destruction. Even at my distance, it buffeted my weakened body.

I tensed against the shock and did my best to keep my eyes open, which is how I saw that Administrator's bolt of lightning erupted into millions of tiny tributaries.

Baaaam!! A peal of thunder accompanied the flying sparks, which in turn created their own, much smaller explosions around the room. And even through the tremendous deluge of energy that it shattered, the sword flew on. The white surface of its blade was covered in fine cracks, and pieces began to fall off. They were parts of Eugeo's body, pieces of his very life.

"Eugeo!!" I screamed, my voice lost in the storm.

"Boy…!!" The smile was gone from Administrator's lips.

The white greatsword reached the source of the lightning at last. Its point hit the needle end of the rapier right on the nose.

An ultra-high-pitched resonance arose, shaking the isolated chamber. For a few moments, Administrator's silver rapier—the source of her godly power—and the white blade that was the fusion of Eugeo and the Blue Rose Sword grappled for supremacy. It looked like total stillness, but I could feel on my skin that this was only the precursor to the coming wave of destruction.

What happened next passed as though it were happening in slow motion.

Administrator's rapier shattered into tiny pieces.

The white greatsword split in two, spraying motes of light.

The front end of the blade shot off, spinning, and silently sliced Administrator's right arm clean off at the shoulder.

The image burned itself into my retinas until sound and vibration finally caught up.

Sacred resources burst forth from the shattered rapier and exploded in a colorful array that engulfed the room.

"Eugeooooooo!!"

Again, my scream was swallowed by the storm that buzzed and squealed like analog static. An oncoming shock wave smashed into my body as it hurtled toward the southern windows. I just barely managed to take cover behind one of the giant swords stuck into the ground that had been part of the golem just minutes ago.

When I could at last stand again, I saw Administrator standing on the ground on her own two feet, clutching her shoulder with her remaining hand…and two large shards of metal at her feet.

Eugeo's broken sword still contained a faint trace of its glow. But even as I watched, it was growing weaker, pulsing like a beating heart, until it disappeared.

The pieces of the white sword began to lose their sense of being, gradually reverting to human form.

The piece from the tip to the middle of the blade became the legs.

And the part including the guard and hilt became the torso and head.

Eugeo was clutching the crystal prism to his chest, his eyes shut. His flaxen hair and milky skin were back to their full, solid texture.

Then, the cross sections where his body was split in two erupted with blood, immediately flooding Administrator's bare feet.

"Ah......ah........."

The sound that croaked from my throat came to my ears as though from a very far distance.

The entire world lost color, lost smell, lost sound. Everything paled.

In the midst of this existence without sensation, only the color of the blood that continued to spill out had any vivacity to it. Something sparkling descended right next to Eugeo, who was lying in a crimson sea.

It landed and stuck in the liquid, sending a ripple outward—a slender blue-silver longsword, the Blue Rose Sword. I thought it was unharmed, but only for a moment; it promptly shattered, the pointed half of the sword breaking apart into ice crystals.

Without its support, the handle half of the sword tipped over and landed next to Eugeo's face. It sent up a splash of blood flecks that hit Eugeo's cheek, only to roll back down his skin.

I managed a few wobbling steps before I fell to my knees. With glassy eyes, I clutched my own sides, clinging to what warmth of Cardinal's body still resided in my arms. But that faint heat did nothing to fill the growing void within me. It was like my mind, my body, and even my soul were going hollow.

Let's end this already.

The thought rose from the emptiness like a bubble and popped.

We—no, I—had lost, in every sense of the word.

My one single reason for being in this place was to help free Eugeo's soul into the real world. Instead, he'd sacrificed himself to protect me, and I was powerless, on my hands and knees—the man who would simply log out to reality when he died in the Underworld.

I just want to fade out, to vanish from the world. I don't want to see any more, hear any more.

All I prayed for was my own obliteration.

But the Underworld was its own reality, and its master was not a program designed to stop once you hit the bad ending.

As she stood in the sea of blood, Administrator's pale, featureless beauty took on the slightest bit of color, which vanished just as quickly. Her gorgeous voice brushed aside the silence of the room.

"I have not suffered such injury in two hundred years. Since my fight with Lyserith."

It almost seemed like there was a note of praise, of admiration, in her voice.

"In terms of priority, Eugeo's converted sword shouldn't have been able to match my Silvery Eternity. I'm surprised at the result. I suppose it was my mistake not recognizing that his sword wasn't metallic in nature."

Drops of blood dripped from her right shoulder, creating more ripples in the puddle at her feet. She caught one in her left palm, converted it to light elements, and rubbed it on the wound. Instantly, the severed cross section sealed over into smooth skin.

"Well," she said, turning her mirror eyes and their long lashes toward me now that she was done with her emergency treatment, "I'll admit that I'm a bit surprised that you were the one who lasted this long, little boy. I'm mildly curious as to why you came here without administrator privileges…but I've also grown tired of this. I will ask the one from the *other side* about how this came to be later. For now, I'll let your blood and screams round out this confrontation."

She began to stride gracefully forward, betraying no sign that she was suffering from her severed arm. She stepped over Eugeo's split body and proceeded toward me, leaving bloody footprints on the bare marble floor.

As she walked, she reached out sideways, and something white flew up from the ground behind her. It was a slender right arm—the limb that Eugeo's sword had cut off her.

I thought she was going to reattach it to her shoulder, but instead, she lifted it up to her face, holding it by the wrist, and blew on it. Instantly, the arm was wreathed in purple light, shuddering mechanically as it underwent matter conversion.

What appeared was a silver longsword, simple in design but beautifully elegant. Its finish wasn't the perfect unbroken mirror that the rapier's was, but given the fact that it was using the arm of the most powerful person in the world as its resource, I was certain that the power it contained was more than enough to separate my head from my shoulders.

Death approached on quiet footsteps. I awaited it from my knees.

In just a few seconds, the administrator of this world arrived before me, dazzlingly beautiful despite her missing arm, and gazed down at me.

I looked up and met the colorful reflection of her mirror eyes. There was just a hint of mirth in them, and a gentle cast to her voice.

"Good-bye, little boy. Let's meet again someday on the other side."

She raised the sword, which caught the light of the moon.

A blade as sharp as a razor cut a blue arc through space toward my neck.

And then there was a silhouette occupying the space before me.

Long hair fanned through the air.

All I could do was watch as the wounded knight held her arms out wide.

I had seen this before.

Was I going
to repeat
the same
mistake…

…*yet again?!*
The thought flashed into my head, stopping time.

In a monochrome world without sound or color, a number of things happened in quick succession.

A small hand brushed my right arm where it dangled lifelessly.

The cold fear and resignation that consumed my entire being melted just a bit with the warmth of that palm.

The negative thoughts hadn't vanished. But the owner of the hand was telling me that it was okay to admit that weakness.

"You don't have to always win every time. If you lose eventually, if you fall, you just need to connect your heart, your will, to someone else.

"I am certain that is how all of those who shared time with you and moved on felt. Even I.

"Which means you can stand again.

"To protect someone you love."

I was conscious of a mild heat emanating from my body, or perhaps my mind, sending circuits of light into my frozen fluctlight.

From the center of my chest, through my right shoulder, down my arm, into my fingers.

My tense fingertips were suddenly engulfed in a burning heat.

With speed I'd never experienced before, my right hand shot to the handle of my black sword nearby and grabbed it.

Then time flowed once more.

Administrator's sword plunged down at the left shoulder of Alice, who stood with arms outstretched to take the blow for me. The sharp blade ripped the sleeve of the charred knight's uniform and was just about to sink into her pale skin.

I swung my sword as I rose to my feet, and I caught the end of the silver sword just in the nick of time, sending up a shower of sparks. The resulting shock pushed Administrator away from Alice and me.

My free hand slipped around to steady Alice as she fell back against me, while the force of the impact pushed me toward the wall—it took both feet holding firm to prevent a collision. She rested her head against my right shoulder, then turned to look up at me with her blue eyes.

"Oh..." Her cheeks, still ugly and burned from the fire attacks she'd suffered, crinkled into a smile. "You can still move...after all," she whispered.

"...Yeah," I said, giving her as close to a smile as I could manage. "Now leave the rest to me."

"I think...I will."

And with that, Alice fell unconscious and slumped to her knees.

I lowered her to the floor and set her back against the window. I sucked in a deep breath and stood again.

Get some rest and leave this to me. Charlotte, Cardinal, and Eugeo have given their lives for mine...so I'll make sure to pass it on to you.

The one thing that was most important was to get Alice out of this enclosed space somehow. I had to fight this woman and at the very least tie if I couldn't win. Even if that meant losing all my limbs, getting stabbed through the heart, or getting my head chopped off.

I leveled my gaze, keenly aware of these possibilities, and stared at my foe.

Administrator's grin was as faint as ever as she gazed at the hand holding her sword. There was a part of her soft palm that was rubbed red and raw, probably from the earlier shock wave.

"...I'm starting to get truly cross," she said with glacial ferocity. Her mirror eyes, too, were as icy as though frost had gathered on them. "What is wrong with you people? Why do you struggle so hideously for no gain? The outcome of the battle is clear already. What meaning can there be in the process of reaching that foregone conclusion?"

"The process is what's important. The part where you either die crawling or die with a sword in your hand. That's what makes us…human beings."

I closed my eyes and imagined my past self again. The self-image of Kirito the Black Swordsman that I'd kept defining for myself for years. The part of me that could never lose—the curse that said if I ever fell in battle, I'd lose everything I ever had.

But now I needed to free myself from that fear and fixation.

When my eyelids rose, long bangs hung over my eyes. I brushed them away with a gloved hand and swept my long black coat aside to brandish my longsword.

A short distance away, Administrator raised an eyebrow, then put on a cruel smile like the one she'd worn when she took Cardinal's life.

"That black outfit…You look just like a black knight from the Dark Territory. Very well. If you simply must suffer, then I will ensure that your fate is very, *very* long and torturous. The kind that will make you beg for death's merciful release."

"That won't be enough to atone for my stupidity," I muttered, dropping my stance and keeping my eyes on the tip of the silver sword in her left hand.

I'd seen plenty of Administrator's superlative power with sacred arts today, but given that her rapier—apparently named Silvery Eternity—was broken, I assumed she could no longer use that valuable resource as a power reserve to execute her rapid-fire arts. It was why she'd had to convert her own severed arm into this sword.

Sword-on-sword fighting was exactly what I wanted, but her skill was a total unknown. I assumed that, like the Integrity Knights, she would gravitate toward major single-attack skills, but if my fight against Alice on the eightieth floor had taught me anything, it was that this wasn't the weakness it might sound like.

My weapon's priority value was probably the lower of the two, so if our swords clashed enough, my already-damaged black sword would break. I had to keep close and try to seize victory with a combination attack, something that Administrator wouldn't know about.

With that in mind, I lowered my center of gravity farther, ready to charge. I slid my right foot forward and pulled my left back, tensing them against the hard floor.

For her part, Administrator coolly raised her sword high behind her head. As I'd suspected, she was using a stance of the traditional High-Norkia style. The attack that would be unleashed was certain to be so fast and heavy that I couldn't shrug it off with a deflection. I had to avoid it entirely and get past her defense.

"…!"

I sucked in a deep breath, tensing my stomach.

The instant I saw her sword waver, I leaped off the floor.

My enemy's sword glowed blue. Detecting that it was the sword skill known to me as Vertical, I pushed harder off my left foot, veering my course right. Vertical was as straight as the name suggested, which made it difficult to aim at targets fleeing to the sides.

The blue trail of the silver sword approached at terrifying speed. I turned to my left, trying desperately to make myself a small target and get past the blade. The end of my coat flapped wide and was severed clean off.

I dodged it!

Next I pushed off my right leg, reversing the sideways drift of my progress, and pulled back my sword…

But the shine in Administrator's sword did not vanish.

"…?!"

As I yelped in shock, her sword completely ignored all inertia and bounced back with a speed that made no sense. There was no way I could avoid it. Instead, I pushed my sword forward, trying to get it into the path of the swing.

Gyaiiing! A cloud of sparks burst with the tremendous impact. I'd successfully blocked the attack, but the pressure was so intense that I felt my right wrist creak. The momentum was strong enough that I had to jump backward to keep from losing my balance. I could use footwork to dodge her upward swing and throw in a counter—

—but once again, her skill with the sword surpassed my imagination.

After tracing a V shape back to an upright position, her sword again roared downward. My weight was held forward, so I couldn't evade the third attack and caught a shallow slice on my left breast. It was only a scratch, but worse than the pain was the fear and shock that jolted through my body.

If the sword skill Administrator was using was the one I knew, then trying to dodge or half-heartedly block it would only get me killed.

"Yaaaah!!" I roared to dispel my fear, activating a sword skill from a posture that wasn't really meant for it. It was the single diagonal slash Slant.

This time my expectations were dead-on, and Administrator's sword practically teleported upward to an overhead position before striking for a fourth time, its deadliest blow yet.

My black sword met the silver one as it came straight down. The special light effect that happened when two sword skills clashed lit up our faces.

The fourth of a four-attack combination couldn't be neutralized with a normal single skill. Fortunately for me, Administrator didn't have her right arm now. Her balance was off, and the slash slipped to the left as it descended.

Gyarinnng! When our swords separated, this time I leaped purposefully outside of swing range.

I touched the cut on my chest and came away with a bit of red on my fingers. It wasn't enough damage to need healing from sacred arts, but I was less concerned with my own flesh than I was horrified about the vivid slice across my leather coat, which was much higher quality than it looked—although it was produced only through the sheer power of my imagination.

Since I was left speechless, Administrator took it upon herself to describe what she had done.

"That was the One-Handed Sword's four-part sword skill Vertical Square...wasn't it?"

There was a brief mental lag before my mind fully processed the meaning of what I'd just heard.

She was correct about the name of the attack. But...

Sword skill.

She'd said the proper name.

Yes, sword skills did exist in the Underworld, just as they did in old *SAO*. But here, they were "ultimate techniques," and their dramatic effects were seen not as active system assistance but as simply the power unlocked from the sword once the user had undergone enough training.

But those techniques these humans used were limited to single-attack skills like Vertical, Cyclone, and Avalanche. It was how I'd won so many duels and battles with my Aincrad-style continuous blade, and I assumed that it would be my only chance at victory here in the final battle, too.

But if Administrator could utilize sword skills *and* execute combination skills of four parts or more, then my advantage was gone.

I inched backward, consumed by confusion and panic—and then I caught sight of Eugeo's maimed body. Blood was still seeping from where he'd been cleaved in half. He had minutes at best before his life ran out.

That beset me with even more to worry about. I needed to think.

Eugeo had been turned into an Integrity Knight, which had temporarily blocked his memory and caused him to fight me. So she must have done a pass on his memories when she did the Synthesis Ritual. In other words, it was possible that she'd scooped the name and movement of Vertical Square from Eugeo's memories.

If that was correct, then Administrator could do One-Handed Sword skills only up to mid-level expertise. I'd never shown my partner the highest skills, after all.

So if I used an attack with over four parts, I still had a chance. The highest of One-Handed Sword skills was actually ten swings in total. And this wasn't the time to be holding back.

I opened my stance and shifted the way I held my sword, and Administrator took note of this and giggled.

"Oh…you've still got that feisty look in your eyes? Very good. Then show me a bit more fun, little boy."

Despite losing one arm, and the major damage to life value that entailed, the pontifex never seemed anything less than confident and in control. I didn't rise to the bait; I just sucked in a deep breath and held it.

The mental image of the sword skill burned into my body and memory came flooding back, vivid and fresh. Already, my sword was beginning to glow with a pale effect.

From the right, it swung around in a circle until it was directly overhead.

"Haaaah!!" I screamed, activating the highest-level One-Handed Sword skill, Nova Ascension.

My body blazed through the air at an impossible speed, pushed by an invisible force. The first blow of the skill was a quick high slice that could get the jump on just about any other skill. No other longsword skills were faster.

Half a second until my slice caught Administrator's left shoulder.

My senses were so accelerated that passing through time was akin to moving through a viscous jelly.

The tip of the silver longsword pointed right at me.

Silver steel shone in a cross shape.

Dak-ka-ka-ka-ka-ka!! Six light-speed thrusts riddled my body, first vertically, then horizontally.

"Guh......"

Blood shot from my mouth.

My ten-move combo, its first attack interrupted, simply vanished into the air as the ice-blue glow around my blade dispersed.

I couldn't even register what had happened, much less theorize how it had happened. Bewildered by pain and shock, I stumbled backward, staring at Administrator's sword as it pulled free from my stomach.

Six consecutive thrusts.

There was no such skill in the One-Handed Sword category.

Hot blood was gushing from small holes in my shoulders, chest, throat, and stomach. The strength went out of my knees, and I thrust my sword into the ground in an attempt to stay upright.

Administrator neatly stepped back to avoid the splashing blood and covered her mouth with the blade of her sword, which suddenly appeared to be much thinner.

"Ha-ha-ha-ha...Too bad, little boy." The beautiful pontifex's lips curled upward in mocking fashion over the fierce edge of the sword. "That was the six-attack rapier skill Crucifixion."

No way.

I had never shown Eugeo that move. More importantly, I could never *use* that move. The most I'd done was see it used a few times all the way back in Aincrad.

I felt the world warping around me. Unless it was actually *me* that was warping. I was struggling to find an answer that described the impossible situation I was facing.

Did she peer into my memories? Did she steal that move from my fluctlight...? And if so, does that mean she perfectly executed a skill that I myself had nearly forgotten...?

"That can't be...," I croaked, in a voice that didn't even sound like my own. "That's impossible..."

My teeth creaked with the pressure of my grinding jaw. I yanked my sword out of the ground, trying to forget an anger that I didn't understand and the fear that refused to release me from its clutches. I tensed my legs, taking a wide, firm stance despite my weakness.

My left hand went out front, and my right hand pulled in close. This was the stance for Vorpal Strike, the single-attack skill that had defeated Chudelkin.

The distance between us was five yards. Well within my range.

"Raaaah!!" I bellowed from deep in my gut, trying desperately to draw on more of the imagination power that had recently wilted. My sword glowed a ferocious crimson color where it rested on my shoulder. It was the color of blood—of naked intent to kill.

In response, Administrator stretched her legs front and back, sank down, and, like I had, smoothly moved her rapier over to her right side. There she paused.

As if just to prove that my eyes hadn't been playing tricks on me seconds earlier, her slender rapier changed shape again. It was wider and thicker now. One sharp edge, long and smoothly curved. Why, it was just like a...

No. No more thoughts. Just rage.

"*Ruoaaahh!!*" I bellowed with animalistic fury and swung.

"Hsst!!" spat Administrator with a short but sharp hiss. The sword at her right side shone bright silver.

It was faster than the straight-line Vorpal Strike and beautifully curved. Her abrupt motion slashed across my chest.

A brief instant later, an impact like a giant's fist smashed me backward. I flew high through the air, much of my remaining life spraying into the air as a red mist.

With her left arm held in place at the end of her swing, Administrator spoke so quietly that I barely heard her.

"Single-attack katana skill Zekkuu."

I didn't recognize that sword skill—but I had to guess that it meant Severed Void.

It was more than shock. I felt like the world itself was crumbling around me as I crashed to the floor. Blood splashed everywhere at the impact.

But it wasn't *my* blood. I'd fallen into the frighteningly large pool of blood that flooded from the two halves of Eugeo's body. My body was frozen, leaving only my eyes capable of movement. I strained them as far as they could go to see Eugeo's top half lying right nearby.

My partner of two years was facing my direction, his skin pale and eyes closed. Little bits of blood still seeped from the grisly wound. Whether his life was already gone or on the verge of running out, it was clear that he wouldn't be regaining consciousness like this.

Only one thing was clear: I had wasted the life that he'd given his to keep alive.

I couldn't beat her.

Not in sacred arts, of course, but not in sword battle, either. She was far superior to me in every way.

There was no way I could know how she'd learned such a wide variety of sword skills. At the very least, it was clear she hadn't gotten them from Eugeo's memories nor my own.

Sword skills weren't a part of the basic Seed package that the Underworld was built upon. The only game that used them was *ALfheim Online*, which was built into the old *SAO* server. But there was no way that the Rath engineers who'd built the Underworld, much less Administrator herself, would have stolen the sword-skill system from the *ALO* server.

Any further conjecture was pointless. Even if I discovered the truth somehow, nothing about it would change the obvious reality of my situation.

Charlotte's sacrifice, Eugeo's determination, Alice's resolution... and Cardinal's last will. And all I'd achieved with them was...

"Yes. That's the face I like to see."

A voice like a frozen blade caressed my neck. Administrator walked, barefoot and languid, across the marble floor toward me.

"I suppose people from the other side must have richer expressions. I wish I could save that despair of yours for all eternity."

She chuckled to herself. "And while I assumed fighting with swords would be a terrible bore, I have to say, it's not bad. You get to feel yourself inflicting that agony upon the opponent. Since we're doing this, I want you to try a little harder, boy. I want to have more fun with you, slicing you to pieces, starting with your fingers and toes."

...*Do your...worst*, I mouthed. *Hurt me, torture me, kill me...*

At least make sure that before I vanish from this world, I suffer ten times, a hundred times, worse than Eugeo and Cardinal.

I lost the strength to speak. Even the hand still stuck to the handle of my black sword was about to lose its grip...

Until just then, when I heard a whisper at my ear.

"This isn't...like you. To just...give up."

It was a halting voice, one about to fade away forever—but one I would never mistake for another.

My eyes rolled upward again. My mind was a blank.

Green eyes, so familiar and comforting they made me want to cry, looked back at me through barely lifted lids.

"Eu...geo," I gasped. My partner gave me a faint smile.

When the Sword Golem had nearly sliced through my stomach, I couldn't move from the pain and terror. But what I'd suffered was nothing next to Eugeo. He was severed clean through—bones, organs, everything. The agony should have been enough to utterly destroy his fluctlight. And yet...

"Kirito," Eugeo said, his voice stronger this time, "I remember...when they took Alice away...how I couldn't move...But you...you were so brave at that young age...standing up to the Integrity Knight like that..."

"...Eugeo..."

It was immediately clear to me that he was referring to when Alice had been taken away from Rulid Village eight years ago. But I hadn't been there at the time. At first, I thought he was confusing it with some other memory, but the look in his green eyes was so crystal clear and lucid that it obliterated any doubts I had that he was telling the truth.

"...So this time...I'm going...to give you that push. Go on, Kirito...I know you can...stand again. You can stand...as many times...as it..."

His right hand twitched. Through the tears that flooded my eyes, I saw his fingers scoop up a piece of blue-silver metal from the sea of blood—the handle of the Blue Rose Sword.

Amid the pool of his own lifeblood, Eugeo squeezed the handle of the sword, which had lost its blade, and closed his eyes. A warm orange glow abruptly engulfed the area. The red sea beneath us shone and pulsed.

"What did you—?!" Administrator raged. But the invincible overlord covered her face with her remaining hand and backed away, almost as though she was afraid of the orange light.

The sea of blood grew brighter and brighter, until it was a blanket of tiny lights that floated off the ground all at once. The levitating motes then descended and began to swirl, funneling down into Eugeo's sword.

A new blade began forming out of the cracked base of the sword.

Matter conversion.

This was a miracle that should only have been possible for the two managers of this world. My breath caught in my throat. A fearsome roil of emotions surged in my chest, bursting out of me in the form of a fresh wave of tears.

Soon the Blue Rose Sword was its old length again. The fine carving of the rose that was its namesake was now a deep-red color. The blade, guard, grip—everything was turning a brilliant red.

With trembling arms, Eugeo held out the beautiful weapon—now more like the "Red Rose Sword"—to me.

Despite having no sensation in it a moment ago, my left hand extended toward the sword, as though pulled by it, and closed around both Eugeo's hand and the weapon handle.

Energy instantly surged deep into my body.

I didn't believe it was sacred arts.

This was the power of Eugeo's will itself. Pure Incarnation power.

I felt the resonance of the soul from his fluctlight to mine, crossing the boundary of worlds.

His hand went limp and left the sword to me, then fell to the floor. Through his faintly grinning lips, from his mind to mine, came a few short words.

"Now stand, Kirito. My friend...My...hero..."

The pain of the wounds all over my body vanished.

The cold emptiness at the center of my breast evaporated in the midst of blazing heat.

I stared at the side of Eugeo's face, his eyes now closed, and whispered, "Yes...I will stand for you. As many times as it takes."

Just seconds ago my arms felt no sensation whatsoever. Now I held them high, black sword in one hand and red sword in the other, and propped myself up off the floor with the blades to get to my feet.

My body did not want to listen. My legs trembled, and my arms felt as heavy as lead. Still, I managed to walk, step by agonizing step.

Administrator stopped averting her face as I approached, and she stared me down with white-hot fury in her eyes.

"...Why?" she demanded, her voice deep and distorted with a metallic edge. "Why do you foolishly resist your fate?"

"...That's why...," I replied hoarsely. "Resisting is the only reason I'm here right now."

I didn't stop walking, despite the many times I nearly toppled over. I just kept moving.

The swords I was holding were unbelievably heavy. But the weight of their existence gave me strength and willed my legs to keep moving.

In the long, long past, in a different world than this one, I had engaged in battles of life and death with two swords, just like this. This was the real me...the real Dual-Bladed Kirito.

Again, the power of my memory, my vision, overwrote reality, and the black coat that was sliced to pieces here and there became whole again. The bodily damage I'd suffered wasn't gone, but whatever my remaining life value was now didn't matter. As long as I could move and swing my swords, I could fight.

Administrator, eyes blazing with fury, took a step back. A second later, she realized that she had retreated, and her white features took on all the wrath of some demon god.

"...How dare you." Her lips didn't even move. The words just rippled her mouth like heat haze. "This is my world. I will not stand for an uninvited intruder acting this way. Kneel. Expose your neck. *Acquiesce!!*"

The air rumbled, and an aura of darkness rose from the pontifex's feet, swirling in many layers. The silver sword shifted from a katana back to a longsword, and she pointed it, shrouded in darkness, right at my face.

"...Wrong," I said, planning for this to be my final statement. I stopped just before the range of her sword skills. "You are merely a plunderer. One who does not love the world, nor the people who live in it...has no right to be called a ruler!!"

I took a stance. The Red Rose Sword in my left hand went in front, and the black sword in my right went to the rear. I pulled back my left leg. I lowered my waist.

Administrator slowly brandished the silver sword, raising it overhead. Her pearly lips uttered a phrase she was very familiar with, this time in the most menacing way.

"To love is to rule. I love all. *I rule all!!*"

The silver sword grew larger, overflowing with thick darkness. Instantly, the blade was the size of a two-handed sword, its black aura mixed with streaks of brilliant red. Then the hefty weapon came hurtling furiously downward. That was the High-Norkia technique Mountain-Splitting Wave—otherwise known as the Two-Handed Sword skill Avalanche.

That attack was the symbol of the Underworld's nobility and had caused hell for me and Eugeo on many occasions. I blocked it with the intersection of my two swords: the Dual Blades defensive skill Cross Block.

"*Gahhhh!*" I bellowed, summoning all my strength to knock back the enemy's weapon. The pontifex's eyes seemed to widen just a bit.

"Enough tricks!" she shouted, jumping back a step. She steadied her weapon, which was back to being a normal longsword again, at shoulder height.

I pulled back my black sword to an equivalent position on my right. Matching vibrations thrummed from both our swords, like combustion engines overlapping and harmonizing. Black and silver swords shone crimson.

Administrator and I leaped at the same time, activating the same sword skill simultaneously: Vorpal Strike.

Like two sides of a mirror, our swords pulled back like arrows, held for an instant to glow twice as bright, then shot forward.

The tips of the two swords followed straight lines, brushing just the tiniest bit before they passed each other.

With a heavy jolt, my right arm was cut clean off below the shoulder.

But likewise, my sword severed Administrator's left arm at the joint.

Two arms, each holding a sword, soared through the air, spraying red.

"Damn youuuu!!"

Administrator was now armless, and her eyes burned with rainbow fires. Her long silver hair stood on end like a living creature, waving in the air in countless locks. The ends of those bunches of hair turned to sharp needles that bore down on me.

"Not yet!!" I roared, sending crimson light jetting down the length of the Red Rose Sword still held tightly by my left hand.

The second blow of the Dual Blades Vorpal Strike, something that would've been impossible in Aincrad, broke through the swarm of silver hair—

—and sank deep into Administrator's chest.

A sensation unbelievably heavy and solid rang in my palm. A feeling so vivid, so harrowing, that I forgot all about the pain of being stabbed by the rapier, or being sliced by the katana, or losing my arm to the longsword.

The edge of the blade sliced through Administrator's smooth skin, broke her breastbone, and blasted her heart behind it—sensations that I was painfully cognizant of.

I had destroyed a human life. It was an act I'd been terrified of since I came to the understanding that the people of this world had true human fluctlights. I'd felt that fear when I used my sword skill on Chudelkin, too.

But in this one instance, I didn't have an ounce of hesitation. Cardinal had left the future in our hands, and faltering was not an option.

And for the sake of the proud overlord Administrator, too.

I had only a second to indulge in that kind of thinking.

The Red Rose Sword, buried deep within her breast, shone with a light far more powerful than that of the sword skill itself. The blade, constructed from the resource of Eugeo's own blood, twinkled as if it were a piece of a star.

And in the next instant, all the resources burst—causing a gigantic explosion.

Her eyes were bulging as far as they could go, a silent scream erupting from her mouth. All over the most beautiful naked body in the world, fine lines of light spread and burst forth.

An explosion of pure energy ballooned outward, swallowing everything in its midst.

I got tossed up like cotton fluff and slammed into the southern window. When I bounced off it and hit the floor, I could feel the blood gushing out of the wound on my right shoulder.

It was a wonder that I still had that much blood to lose after all the cuts I'd taken already. For a moment, I wondered whether my life really was going to run out, but there was still work to be done. I had to live at least a bit longer.

I glanced at the sword in my hand. The blade was back to its previous half length, and the rose decoration on the side was blue once more. I placed the sword on the ground and squeezed my right shoulder hard.

Strangely enough, white light flooded from my palm and sank into the wound, warm and soothing, without needing any command. The instant I felt the bleeding had stopped, I let go. The spatial resources had to be nearly dried up, and I didn't want to waste what was left.

I put my left hand, not glowing anymore, on the floor and pushed myself up.

Then I gasped.

Through the floating little bits of lights that I assumed were the aftermath of the explosion, I saw the silver-haired girl—who should've been obliterated into nothing—standing unsteadily on her own two feet.

It was a wonder that her shape was still human at all. Her arms were gone, a gaping hole sat in the middle of her chest, and there were cracks running all over her skin, as if it were porcelain that was ready to break.

And what flowed from that multitude of wounds was not blood.

Something like silver and purple sparks was sputtering and shooting from her body, filling the air. It was a sight that made it seem like the people she'd turned to swords weren't the only ones whose bodies had been changed—hers didn't seem to be biological, either.

Her melted-platinum hair had lost its shine and hung in a bedraggled state. Through the shadows they cast, I saw her lips move, emitting a croak that I could just barely hear.

"...Not just one...but both swords...not made of metal... hah...ha-ha..." She laughed, shoulders bobbing like a broken puppet. "What a surprise...what an unexpected...outcome...I've suffered a wound...that I cannot heal...even by gathering up the remaining...resources here..."

I had been in the grips of a nightmare vision of Administrator healing herself instantly and entirely, but now I was able to exhale at last.

The supreme ruler, on death's door now, slowly turned her collapsing body. She tottered forward like a toy losing its battery charge, sparks shooting from various parts of her body.

She was heading for the north end of the room. There was nothing I could see there, but she must've been going for something. Whatever it was, I had to finish her off before she reached it.

With desperate effort, I got to my feet and stared carefully at her backside, which seemed smaller than before. I followed, dragging my foot, my gait even more awkward than hers.

She was a good twenty yards in front of me and heading for a specific spot. But without any resources here, she shouldn't have been able to escape this isolated space. Cardinal had said it was not easy to patch such a thing back together, even if separated for only a few minutes. And Administrator hadn't denied it.

Many seconds later, she came to a stop in an empty spot. But when she turned around, naked and wounded, there was a grin on her face. She looked at me, trying to catch up to her.

"Heh-heh...At this point, I have no...choice. It is a bit...earlier than I planned...but I suppose...I will be...going now."

"Wh...what are you...?"

...*saying*, I wanted to ask. But Administrator cut me off by stomping the floor with her cracked right leg.

There was a strange circular symbol on the burned carpet beneath her feet. It was extremely similar to the spot marking the location of the levitating platform behind me, but something about this one was different.

This circle, about a foot and a half across, was the familiar purple color of the user interface.

The floor vibrated subtly and rose up to reveal...a white marble pillar.

And a laptop computer sitting atop it.

"Wha...?"

I was so stunned that my legs gave out and I fell to my knees.

It wasn't exactly the same as a real-life laptop. The body looked like some kind of partially translucent crystal, and the screen was see-through and faintly purple. It was very, very similar to the virtual system console I saw once in Aincrad.

That was it.

That was the connection mechanism to the outside world I'd been searching for these past two years.

An almost violent urge overtook me, making me scrape the floor with my hand in an effort to move forward. But my progress was devastatingly slow, and my destination was definitively too far.

Without any arms to use, Administrator instead brandished a lock of her silver hair like a living creature to strike at the keyboard. A small window opened on the holo-screen, containing some kind of indicator that began a countdown.

Then a purple pillar of light appeared from the ground where she stood—and Administrator's battered body rose into the air.

At last, she lifted her face and looked directly at me.

Her perfect beauty was in a dreadful state. The left side of her face was badly cracked, and the place where her eye should be was filled with impenetrable darkness. The lips that gleamed a shade of pearl looked more like paper now—but the thin smile on them still carried an arctic frostiness to it.

Her intact right eye narrowed, and she cackled. "Hah...hah...So long, little boy. Until...we meet again. In...your world...this time."

At last, I understood what it was she was intending to do.

She was trying to escape into the real world.

She wanted to escape the Underworld, with its absolute limit on existence in the form of her life value, so that she could preserve her fluctlight—the exact same way I had hoped to do with Eugeo's and Alice's souls.

"W-wait!!" I cried, crawling for all I was worth.

If I were her, I'd destroy the console just before the moment of escape. If she did that, then all hope would be lost.

Administrator's naked form climbed, slowly but surely, up the ladder of light.

Her smiling lips mouthed a silent farewell.

Good-b—

But before they formed the final vowel, someone who had crawled to the base of the console without either of us noticing screamed.

"Your Holiness...Pleaaaase! Take me with youuuuu..."

Prime Senator Chudelkin.

The clown whose torso my sword skill had penetrated, and who'd been scrapped for good by Administrator, was right there all of a sudden, his bloodless face twisted in desperation, reaching upward with fingers bent like claws.

His small body burst into searing flames. Through some kind of sacred arts—or perhaps Incarnation—Chudelkin turned his own body into a flaming clown this time and began to spiral into the air.

Even Administrator looked shocked, and possibly even frightened. Just as she was nearly up to the exit of the pillar of light, Chudelkin's flaming hands caught the pontifex's feet.

His thin, elongated clown's body wrapped itself around and up her naked form, clinging to her like a snake. The ferocious flames engulfed both of their bodies.

Even her hair caught fire, the pointed ends of it melting away. Her lips twisted, and she screamed in frustration.

"Unhand me! Let go of me...you fiendish ingrate!!"

But Chudelkin's round face only beamed with bliss, as though his master's words had been a confession of her love for him.

"Aaaah...At last...at last I can be one with Your Holiness..."

His short arms clung fiercely to her body. The cracks in the woman's skin turned red with the heat, and small pieces began to fall away.

"I would never...bother with...a hideous clown...like you...!" she screamed. Silver sparks from the pontifex's body mixed with Chudelkin's flames, illuminating the vast chamber.

Chudelkin's body had no form anymore; he was a mass of flame alone, with only a blissful expression left in the middle to utter his final words.

"Ahhh…Your Holiness…my…Adminis…tra…tor…"

And then Administrator's body began to burn from the extremities.

The supreme ruler's face caught on fire, and the fear and rage there vanished. Her silver eyes looked skyward. Even in the moment of her utter destruction, she was unfathomably beautiful.

"……I……my own……world……"

I couldn't hear anything after that.

The wild conflagration rapidly contracted. The flames converted to a platinum flash of light that further contracted and then expanded.

It wasn't quite an explosion. It was more like everything was returned to a state of light that filled the space. There was no sound or vibration, simply the conceptual phenomenon of the oldest living soul in the Underworld perishing, an event that expanded past the walls of this enclosed, isolated space.

The silver light shone and shone for so long that I began to wonder whether the world would ever return to its original state.

But eventually, the light did indeed begin to abate, and color returned to my sight at last.

I blinked several times to clear the tears—surely because of the light that burned my eyes—and I looked closely at the point that had been the heart of the explosion.

I couldn't find a single piece of evidence that the woman and the clown had ever been there. The pillar of light was gone, leaving behind only the marble pedestal sticking up from the floor and the crystal console on top of it.

At last, both logic and intuition told me that Administrator, who had once been a girl named Quinella, was utterly gone. Her life had reached zero, and the lightcube that held her fluctlight was reinitialized. So too, I expected, would be the lightcube of Cardinal, located adjacent to it.

"…So…it's over…," I mumbled from my knees, hardly realizing the words were coming from my own mouth. "……Was this…the right thing to do…Cardinal…?"

There was no answer.

But it seemed as though a tiny breeze from the depths of my memory brushed my cheek.

It was the scent of Cardinal when we'd made bodily contact on the floor of the Great Library—old books, candle wax, and sugar candy, mixed into one.

I wiped my tears aside with my left arm and realized my sleeve had reverted from the leather coat back to my black shirt. Then I turned to crawl toward Eugeo, who was nearly at the center of the room.

My partner's brutally severed body continued dripping blood at long intervals, drop by agonizing drop. He had minutes to live at best.

When at last I reached his side, my first idea was to stop the bleeding by picking up his lower half and fitting it back against the spot where he'd been sliced. Then I placed my palm against the cut and imagined that healing light.

The glow that appeared below my hand was so faint that I had to squint to see it. Still, I pushed it against him anyway, hoping it would seal the cut.

But the red liquid that was Eugeo's life itself continued to seep from his halves. The priority of my healing was definitively inadequate for the severity of his wound, I knew. But I waved my hand around anyway and shouted, "Stop...just stop! Why won't you work?!"

The power of imagination determined everything in the Underworld. If I just wished hard enough, I could make any miracle happen. Right?

I prayed, begged, wished so hard that I could've wrung every last drop of strength from my soul.

But still, another drop of Eugeo's blood dripped from his wound. And another.

The overwriting ability of one's imagination could affect only the locations and appearances of objects. It couldn't alter values like priority level, durability, and other numerical attributes. I was aware of this fact, but I didn't want to acknowledge it. Not now.

"Eugeo...come back to me, Eugeo!!"

I stuck my wrist into my mouth, ready to bite it off. I knew it wouldn't be enough, but in the moment, I needed to give all my available resources to him. Even if it meant that both of us lost our lives in the end.

My canines sank into my skin, ready to tear flesh and blood loose, when I heard a faint whisper call my name.

"......Kirito."

I looked up with a start.

Eugeo's eyelids were just barely lifted. He was smiling.

His face was paler than the moonlight itself, and his lips were totally bloodless. It was obvious that his life was continuing to drain away. But his green eyes were the same as when I first met him, gentle and warm and bright.

"Eugeo...!" I exclaimed. "Hang on—I'll heal you right now! I'm not letting you die...It's not going to happen!"

I put my wrist in my mouth again. But then a hand, cold as ice yet as warm as a patch of sunlight, closed over my wrist and squeezed gently.

"Eu...," I grunted, but Eugeo kept his grip. From his lips tumbled an English phrase I'd taught him back at the academy, a little secret mantra just between the two of us.

"Stay cool...Kirito."

"...!"

I took a ragged, quivering breath. I had told Eugeo that it was a parting phrase. I hadn't taught it to him so that I could hear him say it here and now. Absolutely not.

I shook my head over and over, but Eugeo kept whispering: "It's...all right. It's meant...to be this way...Kirito."

"What are you talking about? Of course it's not all right!" I yelped. Eugeo just kept smiling. He almost seemed satisfied.

"...I...fulfilled...my role...to play...This is where...our paths... split apart..."

"That's not true! I don't believe in fate!! I don't accept that answer!!" I screamed, sobbing like a child. Eugeo wisely shook his head. Even that tiny gesture should have required intense concentration, but he showed no signs of suffering.

"…If this…hadn't happened…then we would've had to fight each other…both for the sake of Alice. I would fight…to take back Alice's memories…and you would fight to protect the soul of Alice the Integrity Knight…"

I held my breath.

It was the very thing I'd been terrified of, deep down, but chosen not to think about. That when all the fighting was over and it came time to insert Alice Zuberg's memory fragment into Alice the knight's fluctlight, the question would be posed: Was I going to agree to that?

Even now, when the moment came, I had no answer.

Instead, I tearfully hurled it back at Eugeo.

"Then…fight me!! Restore your full strength and fight me!! You're already stronger than I am!! So you need to get back on your feet and fight me…for Alice…!"

But Eugeo's serene smile never wavered. "My sword…is already…broken. Plus…it was…my weakness…that led me to open my heart…to Administrator…and to try to fight you. I have…to pay…for that sin…"

"It's not a sin! You're guilty of nothing!!" I sobbed, grabbing his wrist this time. "You've fought valiantly the whole way! If it wasn't for you, we'd never have beaten Chudelkin or the Sword Golem or Administrator! You have nothing to blame yourself for, Eugeo!!"

"……You…think so…? I…hope so…," he mumbled, eyes full of large tears that ran down his cheeks. "Kirito…I've always… been jealous of you. You were stronger…and more beloved…than anyone…A part of me was afraid…that even Alice…would prefer… W-well, anyway…I finally…understand. Love isn't something…you seek…It's something you…give. Alice…taught me…that…"

He stopped talking and lifted his left hand. His palm, ragged and torn from all the fighting, held a tiny crystal: a translucent, double-ended hexagonal prism. Alice's memory fragment.

The clear prism glowed as it brushed my hand.

The world filled with light.

I no longer felt the hardness of the floor or the pain of my severed arm. A gentle flow carried my soul somewhere distant. Even the terrible sadness engulfing my heart simply melted away in that warm light.

And then...

Something bright and green was waving far overhead.

Sunlight through leaves.

Fresh shoots were spurting out of the tree branches, soaking in the long-awaited spring sun and swaying in the breeze. The smooth black branches rustled as unfamiliar little birds flitted and chased one another around.

"Your hands are idle, Kirito."

The sound of my name yanked my attention down from the branches.

The blond hair of the girl sitting next to me glimmered in the light falling through the leaves. I blinked a few times and shrugged. "Well, you were staring openmouthed at that family of cottonrabbits, Alice."

"I did not have my mouth open!" protested Alice Zuberg, the girl in the blue-and-white apron dress. She lifted what she was holding up to the sunlight.

It was a finely crafted leather sheath for a short sword. The surface had been polished to a shine with an oil rag, and a decorative dragon had been stitched on with white thread. It was a somewhat familiar, rounded dragon, with the tail only half-done, a needle dangling from the end of the unfinished loose thread.

"Look, mine's going to be finished very soon. How's yours coming along?"

I looked down at my knees. Resting there was a short sword carved from a branch of platinum oak, the second-toughest wood in the forest. Old Man Garitta, who knew more than anyone about the forest, had shown me how to carve the iron-tough material, and it had taken me two months to get it to this state. The blade was already finished; I just had to put the finishing touches on the handle.

"I'm further along. Almost done with it," I told her.

Alice grinned and said, "Then let's hurry and finish up the last bit."

"Mmm."

I looked up to the sunlight coming through the branches again. Solus was past the middle of the sky now. We'd been working in our secret spot here all morning, so it seemed like we should probably head back to the village soon.

"Hey...we should get going back. Or we'll get busted," I said, shaking my head.

Alice pouted like a little child. "We're still fine. Let's stay a bit longer...just a bit?"

"Well, fine. But only for a little while, got it?"

We called it a deal and spent the next several minutes absorbed in our work.

"All done!"

"Finished!"

Our voices overlapped, right at the same moment that the grasses rustled and parted behind us. I spun around, hiding what I was holding behind my back.

Standing there and looking bewildered was a boy with soft flaxen hair cut short to keep it under control—Eugeo.

His pure-green eyes blinked, and he said suspiciously, "I didn't see either of you all morning. You've been here the whole time? What are you doing here?"

Alice and I hunched our shoulders and shared a look.

"Well, I guess he figured it out."

"See? I told you. Now it's all for nothing."

"It's not *ruined*. Here, just hand it over."

Alice grabbed the newly finished wooden sword from me and slipped it into her leather sheath neatly—and behind her back.

Then she hopped forward toward Eugeo, gave him a smile as radiant as the sun, and shouted, "It's three days early…but happy birthday, Eugeo!!"

The boy stared wide-eyed at what she offered him: a short sword of platinum oak, in a sheath with white dragon stitching on it.

"Uh…it's…for me…? This incredible thing…?"

All I could do was chuckle now that Alice had stolen the best part of the surprise away from me. "You said the wooden sword your dad bought you is broken, right? So we decided…Look, I know it's not like the real one that your brother has, but *this* wooden sword's better than any you'll find at the general store!"

Eugeo reached out uncertainly and took the short sword in both hands, then arched his back in surprise when he felt its weight. His face broke into a smile just as big as Alice's.

"You're right…this is heavier than my brother's sword! This is amazing…I…I'll take such good care of it. Thanks, you two. This is great…I've never gotten such a wonderful birthday gift before…"

"H-hey…don't cry, man!" I shouted when I saw the shine in the corners of his eyes. He rubbed at his face, claiming that he wasn't crying.

Then Eugeo looked right at me. He smiled again.

All of a sudden, his smile blurred and blotted.

There was an abrupt pain in my chest. A feeling of unstoppable nostalgia, homesickness, and loss. The tears flowed without stopping, soaking my cheeks.

Alice and Eugeo were crying, too, standing side by side.

We all spoke together.

"The three of us lived the same era together."

"Our paths separate here…but our memories remain eternal."

"I will continue to live…within you. So, look…"

The vision of sun and shade vanished, and I was back on the top floor of Central Cathedral.

"So, look…don't cry, Kirito."

Eugeo's arms went limp. His right hand hit the floor, and his left landed on his chest. The prism's glimmering had nearly died out.

The scene that had just played out on the screen of my mind *was* my own memory. I only remembered a single scene, but the truth of it, that Alice and Eugeo and I had been childhood friends who grew up together and were connected by an unshakable bond of friendship, filled my body with a warmth that eased the pain of loss just a bit.

"Yeah...the memories are in here," I sobbed, pressing my fingers into my chest. "They'll be here forever."

"That's right...And it means we'll be friends forever. Where... Kirito, where are you? I can't see you...," Eugeo called, his fading eyes wandering, though the smile never left his face.

I leaned over and clutched Eugeo's head with my one hand. My tears dripped down onto his forehead. "I'm here. I'm right here."

"Oh..." Eugeo was gazing somewhere far into the distance now. His smile looked very satisfied. "I can see it...glittering in the darkness...like stars...The starry sky...that I looked up at... every night...from the foot of...the Gigas Cedar...Just like...the shine...of your...sword..."

His voice was growing clearer, more transparent by the moment. It caressed my very soul.

"In fact...I think your black sword...should be called...the Night-Sky Blade. What do you...say...?"

"Yeah...it's a great name. Thank you, Eugeo."

I clung to my friend's body, which was getting lighter by the second. Our minds were in contact, his final words rippling into the air like a droplet into water.

"Envelop......this...little world...as gently...as the night...... sky......"

The clear liquid trapped in his eyelashes transformed into light and disappeared.

With what little weight he had left, Eugeo leaned back into my arms and slowly closed his eyes.

6

Eugeo was standing in a dark, unfamiliar hallway.

But he wasn't alone.

Holding his left hand was Alice, wearing her blue dress, beaming back at him.

He squeezed her hand a bit harder and told his childhood friend, "I guess…this was for the best."

Alice nodded vigorously, shaking the ribbon that held her golden hair in place. "Yes. We can leave the rest to those two. I'm sure they'll guide the world in the right direction."

"Yeah. So…shall we go?"

"Okay."

Somehow, he was back to his youthful form again. He and the girl his age and height walked hand in hand down the hallway in the direction of the distant light.

And in that instant…

The durability value of the human unit designated NND7-6361 dropped to zero.

Upon receiving that signal, the program that controlled the Lightcube Cluster issued a single order to the cube that held the corresponding fluctlight. The interface faithfully executed its order, reinitializing the praseodymium crystal structure.

Over ten billion cubits of photons glowed at once and dispersed.

A soul named Eugeo, who hadn't lived even twenty years of subjective time, was freed forever from the little cube.

And at the same time, another lightcube located far away from his own was similarly processed.

That lightcube, produced through improper system operation using memories extracted from the soul named Alice Zuberg, was also freed from its crystal prison.

Where the amalgamation of photons that made up those two souls disappeared to was a question no one could answer.

7

I knelt in that exact spot where I'd been, until Eugeo's body and Alice's memory fragment resting on his chest vanished into motes of light, the same way Cardinal's body had.

How long was I there? The next thing I knew, the swirling tempest that represented isolated space outside of the windows was gone, and the full starry sky was back. Over the End Mountains on the far eastern horizon, the faintest bit of violet heralded the coming dawn.

I lifted myself up, mind barely functioning, and approached Alice the knight where she lay.

Alice's wounds were terrible to behold. Fortunately, most of the damage was from her burns and not from blood loss. Her life had stopped its steady decrease. I propped her up with my left hand, and although she didn't wake up, her eyebrows did twitch, and a faint breath exhaled from her lips.

With Alice on my good arm, I slowly, slowly headed for the north end of the room.

At this point, the crystalline system console there, sparkling artificially, was the only object in the room that was undamaged in any way.

I laid Alice down on the floor and hit one of the see-through glowing keys. The monitor lit up, displaying a complex management screen. The user interface was almost entirely in "sacred script"—English—but a few presses of the screen led me to what I sought.

CALL EXTERNAL OBSERVER

I stared at the tab for a while. "Observers"—the ones who created, operated, and watched over this world.

These people, the staffers at the tech start-up named Rath, had lied to me only once—but it was the biggest lie imaginable.

In June 2026 in the real world, which felt like an eternity ago, I'd participated in a long-term continuous test of their next-generation full-dive machine, The Soul Translator, or STL.

The test period was three days. Through the Fluctlight Acceleration (FLA) feature, the subjective time I spent in the VR world would be 3.3 times as long as real time, or ten days in total. At the end of the test, they had blocked my memories of the event to protect company secrets, or so they'd explained to me.

But that was a lie. I hadn't dived into a test environment; they had sent me into the same Underworld I was in now. And it wasn't ten days I spent here. I estimated it was over three hundred times that amount…for a span of ten *years*.

Yes, during that three-day test, I experienced an entire second childhood, from infancy to the age of eleven, in a tiny village at the northern end of the world. I spent every day playing in the mud with my best friends, the flaxen-haired boy and the golden-haired girl, and at the end of each day, we trudged home along the riverbanks to the village, side by side.

Two years ago, when I'd just woken up in this place, I saw a vision of that sunset at the bank of the river in the woods. When fighting against Eugeo, I had a sensation of kids swordfighting. And just now, at the moment of Eugeo's death, I saw the scene about the platinum-oak sword. These things weren't illusions.

They were fragments of the memories that had been deleted, things I had really experienced. I grew up with Eugeo and Alice in the village of Rulid, and I had forgotten all about it until today.

Eugeo and Alice, too, couldn't access their memories of living with me. They both got synthesized by the supreme ruler, but perhaps that memory issue was responsible for both of them recovering their own free will from the process, unlike the other Integrity Knights.

It didn't matter to me anymore *why* Rath would have inserted an outside element like me into their civilization simulation. But there was one thing I couldn't forgive.

I'd been there eight years ago.

I'd been there when Deusolbert had taken young Alice away.

Eugeo had blamed himself for that for years. He'd never stopped regretting that he couldn't save her. And half of that regret should've been mine to shoulder. But I'd forgotten the past...and I'd never understood the depth of Eugeo's suffering until the moment he gave up his life...

"Nn...guh...khf...!"

Bizarre sounds escaped from my throat. I clenched my jaw shut as hard as I could, my molars creaking and groaning with the pressure.

My stiff left hand rose, the fingers trembling, and pressed the button to call an observer. A dialogue box in Japanese appeared with a warning sound.

Performing this operation will fix Fluctlight Acceleration rate at ×1.0. Are you sure?

I hit the okay button without thinking twice.

Instantly, the air around me felt viscous. Sound, light, all sensation extended into the distance, then followed behind me. It was as though my actions and even my thoughts were in super-slow motion for one brief, disorienting moment—and then the sensation was gone.

In the center of the screen was a black window. In the middle of that was a volume meter, just below the blinking words SOUND ONLY.

The meter twitched, producing a rainbow-gradient bar. Then it shot upward, just as a rustling static noise reached my ears.

This was sound from the real world, I sensed.

The world on the "other side," where things were no doubt peaceful and totally unconnected to the madness happening in the Underworld. The real world, where this blood and pain and even death were merely events of interest, at best.

A great storm of numerous emotions that I'd been keeping under control came bursting up from inside me, rocking me where I stood. I leaned toward the monitor and, in as loud a voice as I could manage, called the man who had brought me to this place.

"Kikuoka…Can you hear me, Kikuoka?!"

If my hand could reach Seijirou Kikuoka or any of the other managers right now, I might actually attempt to strangle them to death. Such was the helpless rage I felt as I slammed my left fist against the marble table and screamed, "Kikuokaaaa!!!"

Then a noise came from the screen.

It wasn't a human voice. It was a crisp series of percussions, *tatatak, tatatatak.*

The first thing that popped into my head was a memory from years ago—the sound of automatic submachine-gun fire in the VRMMO called *Gun Gale Online.* But the other side of the screen was just a laboratory for Rath, a small tech start-up. Why would I be hearing that from there?

But then I did hear a human voice. More than one…carrying on a tense, shouted conversation.

"…can't, they've got position in the A6 corridor! I'm pulling back!!"

"Fight them off at A7, then! Give me time to lock the system!!"

There was more rattling. Here and there were sporadic explosions.

What is this…? A movie? Were the staffers streaming a movie in the lab, and was I just picking up the audio from the speakers?

But then an unfamiliar voice said a very familiar name.

"Lieutenant Colonel Kikuoka, it's too late! We're abandoning Maincon and shutting the pressure-resistant barrier!!"

A sharp, rich voice replied, *"Sorry, hold out for two more minutes! We can't lose this place now!!"*

Seijirou Kikuoka. The man who'd brought me to this world.

I'd never heard him under such duress before. What the hell was happening on the other side of the screen?

Are they under attack? Rath? But why...?

Kikuoka spoke again. *"Is the locking process still going, Higa?!"*

The voice that answered him was another one I remembered. That was Takeru Higa, the Rath engineer who'd performed the test dive on me.

"Another eighty...no, seventy seconds to go...Ah...aaaaaah!!"

All of a sudden, Higa's voice turned into a shriek. Something had startled him.

"Kiku!! It's a call from inside! I mean, inside the Underworld!! This is...Ohhh! It's him! It's Kirigaya!!"

"Wh...what?!"

Footsteps approached. Someone grabbed the mic.

"Kirito, are you there?! Are you in there?!"

That was definitely Seijirou Kikuoka. Holding back my confusion, I shouted, "Yeah! Listen, Kikuoka...you monster...What you've done is—!"

"I'll listen to every last name you can call me later! Right now, you need to listen to me!!"

He was in such a pressing panic that I actually stopped in my tracks.

"Listen very carefully, Kirito...You must find a girl named Alice! When you do..."

"Find her...? She's right here!" I shouted back, and now it was Kikuoka's turn to be stunned into silence. Then he rushed back into his explanation, faster than before.

"M-my God...that's a miracle! G-good...Then once this transmission ends, I'm going to return the FLA rate to a thousand. You take Alice and head for the World's End Altar! The internal console you're using now connects directly to Main Control, but that's about to fall!"

"To fall…? What's going on there…?"

"I'm sorry—I don't have time to explain! Listen, to get to the altar, you have to leave the Eastern Gate and head far to the south…"

Then the very first voice I heard came in again, very close by.

"Lieutenant Colonel, I closed the A7 barrier, but that only bought us minutes at……No, wait, oh no! They've started severing the main power line!!"

"Oh man, that's bad! That's real bad!!" shrieked not Kikuoka but Higa. *"Kiku, there'll be a surge if they cut the main power now! The Lightcube Cluster's protected…but the surge will hit Kirigaya's STL in Subcon…It'll fry his fluctlight!!"*

"No…that can't be! There are numerous safety limiters on the STL…"

"But they were all deactivated! He's recuperating, remember?!"

What in the world were they talking about?

What was this about my fluctlight if the power went out?

A split-second silence fell, until Kikuoka broke it.

"I'll handle the locking here! Higa, you take Dr. Koujiro and Asuna and evacuate to the Upper Shaft. Keep Kirito safe!!"

"B-but what about Alice?!"

"I'll raise the FLA rate to its max limit! We can think about the rest later! Right now his protection is paramount…"

I hardly listened to any of the rest of their shouted exchange. One of the names Kikuoka had mentioned struck my mind, rocking it like a storm.

Asu…na?

Asuna's there? At Rath…? But why?

I leaned closer to the console to ask Kikuoka. But before I could say anything, the original voice let out a pitiful scream.

"I can't…They're cutting the power!! The screw propellers are going to stop—all units brace for impact!!"

And then…I saw something strange.

White pillars of light, silently falling from far above and piercing the ceiling of the cathedral.

All I could do was look upward at all the beams of light intersecting on me.

There was no pain, no impact, no sensation of any kind.

But I understood on instinct that I had suffered too much damage to recover from. The light wasn't piercing my flesh; it was piercing my soul itself, it seemed.

Something very important, something that made me *me*, was ripped into pieces and vanished.

Time, space, even memory melted into an empty void.

I simply was…

Even that word lost its meaning.

And just before the ability to think itself was lost, I heard a distant voice.

"Kirito…Kirito!!"

It was a voice so nostalgic I wanted to cry, a sound that was maddeningly precious.

It was…

Whose voice is that…?

(To be continued)

AFTERWORD

Hello, everyone. Thank you for reading *Sword Art Online 14: Alicization Uniting*.

The Alicization arc has gone from *Beginning* to *Running* to *Turning* to *Rising* to *Dividing* to *Uniting*, and this arc marks a turning point for it.

At the end of 2008, when I was having a meeting with my editor about publishing *SAO*, I remember us saying, "Let's make it a goal to publish all the way to the Alicization storyline." It was so far ahead that it didn't seem real at the time, but now I look up and we're at the end of the human realm part of the arc. It's true that time (and the number of volumes) flies...

Warning: The next section covers major spoilers for this book!

Kirito's partner and best friend from Volume 9 to Volume 14, and the other protagonist of this story, Eugeo, has finally left the stage. For a main character of the series, he was surprisingly passive and deferential—during the long journey of leaving the village, joining the academy in the big city, getting arrested, escaping, and climbing the tower, it feels like all he's been doing is chasing after Kirito's lead.

As a matter of fact, when it came to prepping the original web novels for this proper book release, I seriously considered changing Eugeo's fate. In the web novels, Eugeo left the story without ever fully expressing himself and his own wants. So it occurred to me that, given my opportunity to rewrite, he might find himself a new path in the story.

In the end, that didn't happen. When I got to "The Scene" in the revision process, I simply couldn't rewrite the story that was already there. It was almost like Eugeo himself refused to allow me to rewrite his fate. Perhaps that was the last and greatest act of self-advocacy from the man who'd always suppressed himself.

I mentioned the "human realm part of the arc" a moment ago; the Alicization arc will expand further and continue for a bit longer. Many of the characters you know and love from the real-world side will get back into the action, so I hope you stick around to see your favorites!

I'm guessing that by the time this book hits the shelves, the news will already be out that the TV animation series *Sword Art Online II* will begin airing in July. You should really check it out! And once again, I must apologize for being very late to submit this to my illustrator abec and my editor Miki. I'll do better... next volume...!

Reki Kawahara—March 2014